The Secret Lives of Roommates

Gay Awakenings — Book 1

The Secret Lives of Roommates by Joey Mayble
Published by Joey Mayble

This is a work of fiction. Names, characters, places, events and incidents are the products of the author's imagination or are used fictitiously. Any resemblance to actual events or persons, living or dead, is purely coincidental.

Cover designed by GetCovers

Prologue

"Ah, fuck!" Andy groaned and bit down hard on his lip.

Wyatt grinned, "Oh, you like that? Want some more?"

There was a fury of button mashing and swear words carrying through the air as Andy struggled to regain the upper hand on this round of *Street Kombat 7*. He'd been doing so well at first, but Wyatt landed a sequence of tricky combos and almost emptied his health bar completely. In retaliation, Andy resorted to ramming his shoulder into Wyatt's, who was sitting next to him on the couch. Normally, one might call that cheating, but Wyatt's strong, solid figure hardly noticed the attack. He merely laughed and returned the gesture with a nudge of his own which nearly sent Andy—who was decently strong himself—tumbling over the armrest.

"Not fair!" he cried.

"You started it!" Wyatt retorted, a smile evident in his voice.

A few more seconds of furious button smashing continued until finally Wyatt ended the match with a move that Andy had to begrudgingly admit to himself was pretty badass.

He tossed the controller onto the coffee table in front of them and let out a frustrated sigh of defeat. "Dude, I had it. I fucking *had* it!"

"Better luck next time, Andrew," Wyatt smiled sweetly.

Wyatt was the only person in the world who could get away with calling him Andrew. Not even Andy's mom called him that. Ever since he was a kid, he absolutely hated it. But for whatever reason, he'd never minded when Wyatt did it. Admittedly, he didn't do it all the time; he usually only called him Andrew when he was trying to get on Andy's nerves or when Andy was getting on *his* nerves. On rare occasions, though, he would use it when he was being serious about something, like that time during sophomore year when he told Andy that he'd caught his girlfriend

6

kissing some other guy at a party. Andy had been devastated at the time, of course, but found something oddly comforting about being addressed by his full name, which he ordinarily hated. Only Wyatt could pull that off.

"Rematch?" Andy asked.

"Nah, I think I'll quit while I'm ahead. Besides, you obviously need time to practice."

Andy knocked him with his shoulder again, "Oh, shut up." Playing video games was an almost nightly routine for them. They'd both sunk far too many hours into practicing as it was.

Wyatt giggled at Andy's attempt to shove him. Then, he set his controller down also and yawned. "You can have your rematch tomorrow. I'm too tired tonight."

Andy frowned and looked over at the clock on the wall. "It's barely nine o'clock."

"I know. It's just been a long day is all." Wyatt sank down onto the couch, laying his head on the armrest, and draped his long legs casually over Andy's lap. Andy didn't bat an eye; this sort of thing was perfectly normal for them. They were best friends after all—not to mention life-long Gamma Alpha Iota brothers.

They'd met during Rush Week in college and clicked with each other more or less instantly. They were lucky enough to end up in the same fraternity by the end of it, which was a relief for them both. Those first few weeks of college, navigating a new life without any friends at all, can be scary. Not that Andy or Wyatt would've admitted that out loud to anyone. Frat bros didn't talk about that sort of thing. But they didn't need to say anything. They both knew. Even from the beginning, they intuitively understood each other.

"Bad day at work?" Andy asked.

Wyatt scrubbed a hand over his face, "Not particularly. Just same old, same old."

It occurred to Andy then that it was the fourteenth of the month, meaning that tomorrow was payday for Wyatt's company. Being a Junior Payroll Specialist, the second and last week of the month was always the most stressful for Wyatt. No wonder he was as tired as he was. And the rest of the week wouldn't be any better. Once payday passed, Wyatt and his team would be fielding paycheck-related issues and complaints for the next couple of days. With nearly sixteen thousand employees to oversee, it seemed there was always *someone* who fell through the cracks each pay period. Not that it was Wyatt's fault. Simply put, the company was a bit of a dumpster fire.

"I thought you said things were starting to get easier," Andy tried weakly, unsure how else to be helpful.

Wyatt carded a hand through his short sandy blond hair and let out a sigh, "I think I've just started adjusting to the madness is all. Truthfully, I don't think this job is ever going to be easy. The payroll system they use is ancient, and we have to hunt down timesheets from managers every fucking pay period. Some of these men are old enough to be my dad and I swear I feel like I'm babysitting their sorry asses. This definitely wasn't what I pictured myself doing when I got a finance degree."

There was also the not-so-little issue of Sue Ellen, his manager. She was a venomous, impatient woman who had been with the company since Day One when they opened twenty-six years ago. Whenever there was a mistake with someone's paycheck, the blame would fall on the shoulders of her overworked and underpaid team. She never took any responsibility herself despite being the supervisor.

It was only after Wyatt took the job that he learned of her obscenely high turnover right—something that she seemed to take a strange sort of pride in. Since taking the job ten months ago, all four coworkers on Wyatt's team had quit and been replaced at least once.

"Maybe you should start looking for work someplace else. It can't be this bad everywhere."

"Yeah, maybe your right," Wyatt said absently, but Andy didn't think that he would be looking for new jobs anytime soon. There was a distant, hollow look in Wyatt's eyes that made him uneasy.

Then, Wyatt blinked a few times, as if shaking away whatever pessimistic train of thought he'd been riding on, and looked at Andy, "What about you? Any luck with the job hunt?"

Andy dropped his eyes down to his hands which were resting on Wyatt's shins. "Ah, no... No luck." A little bit of color had risen in his cheeks, but Wyatt didn't notice.

"Well, don't throw in the towel. Things will turn up eventually." Wyatt gave him a sad, lopsided smile, and Andy returned it.

"Thanks."

"Do you at least like your job right now?"

The job Wyatt was referring to was a cashier position at an office supply store called Office Haven. Andy had gotten the job about fourth months back out of sheer desperation.

Since graduating from college last year, things had very much *not* been going Andy's way. At first, he'd felt like he had his life together. Thanks to an internship he'd done over the summer between junior and senior year, he already had a good job lined up for him right out of school. He was to start as a Junior Account Executive in July at a trendy tech startup in the city, two hours east of their college town. Wyatt, who didn't have a job waiting for him upon graduating, made the move with him and found his current payroll job by late August.

For a while, things were good. They were both employed, making steady money, and enjoying city life (within their means, of course). Then, Andy's company went belly up just before Christmas, and everyone was laid off. It had taken him completely off guard, and he floundered around frantically looking for a new job. He applied to different places for months and didn't get so much as a single damn nibble. Turned out that having a bachelor's in public relations didn't open up as many doors as he thought it would.

Then, with his already meager savings dwindling, he became *truly* desperate, lowered his expectations a lot, and started applying to minimum wage jobs that he felt overqualified for. Apparently, nobody else thought he was overqualified because not even those gigs were interested in interviewing him. Finally, just as Andy was about to call his parents and pathetically beg for a loan to cover next month's rent, Office Haven reached out.

It was a shit job, but it was a start.

"Um, it's okay," Andy said. "I'm just happy to have a job, y'know? I spent so long without one."

"Yeah, you really had me worried for a while," Wyatt said. "I did the math, and with my current income, I wouldn't be able to cover both of our share of rent *and* make payments on my student loans. I made a spreadsheet and everything."

Andy had to smile. Wyatt was something of an oddity. He was tall and built like a rugby player, but he had a very mathematical mind—hence the degree in finance.

"Wow, you made a spreadsheet?" Andy asked wryly. "You really *were* worried!"

Wyatt laughed and knocked his leg lightly against Andy's chest, "Shut up. You know I love a good spreadsheet." A thought appeared to cross his mind, because he sobered up and added, "If you ever want me to set up one for you to track your own finances and stuff, I'd be happy to."

That was Wyatt's subtle way of saying, *I know you're not making much money right now and that you're stressed. I want to help.*

Andy sighed. "Thanks, dude. I appreciate it, but honestly, seeing my situation spelled out in cold hard numbers might just depress me even more. I don't even want to think about how much interest I've accrued on my student loans right now." Since he lost his job in December, he's had his loans deferred, which meant that the water level of his debt was gradually rising while he was just struggling not to drown.

They sat together in silence, reflecting on their lives.

"Jesus," Wyatt said after a moment. "Who would've thought we'd end up like this?"

Andy gave a rueful smile, "I know. I remember being so excited about graduating. If only I'd known."

Wyatt's eyes were someplace far away. It seemed he was back on that pessimistic thought train again. With that vacant look on his face, he quietly said, "Sometimes I feel like our lives are already over. We're only twenty-three, Andy. How sad is that?"

Andy didn't know what to say. It was the same thought he'd been running from since losing his job back in December. Every day he was worried about making ends meet. Even when he was smiling and laughing about something with Wyatt, the fear of the future never fully went away.

Finally, Wyatt's numb, empty expression was erased by a yawn. "Goodness gracious, I'm going to pass out on this couch if I'm not careful. I need to go to bed."

The corner of Andy's mouth quirked into a small smile. Wyatt was a transplant from Georgia and when he got sleepy, his southern accent came out strong.

Swinging his legs off of Andy's lap, Wyatt stood and stretched. "Goodnight. Be sure to get some practice in before our rematch tomorrow. You need it."

"God, you're so annoying," Andy grinned and playfully stuck out his leg as he passed, trying to trip him. "Goodnight, punk."

When Wyatt's door closed, Andy turned off the video game and switched off the lights in the kitchen. Their apartment was tiny but nice for the price. It was a newer building, and their unit came equipped with a washer and dryer—which was one of the few miracles that Andy could account for in his life currently. On top of that, each of them had their own small *en suite*, which was also a luxury he knew better than to take for granted.

With the lights turned out, Andy went to his room, locked the door, and opened his laptop. A small swarm of butterflies fluttered in his gut. It happened every time he logged into his profile. His *secret* profile.

He'd never had a secret like this before. Not even Wyatt knew about it, and he pretty much knew everything. No, this was something he could never tell anybody.

Upon entering his login credentials, there was the typical welcome banner at the top of the page:

Welcome to FanFrenzy! Where all your FANtasies come true

He clicked on his notifications and saw that he had three new subscribers. He smiled to himself. Every new subscriber brought a small sense of relief. He was slowly but surely digging himself out of the poverty hell he was in.

When he first started working at Office Haven, Andy told himself that this part-time retail job was just a temporary stepping stone while he continued to hunt for better, full-time work elsewhere. However, his hope and determination withered after another couple of months of rejections. He genuinely felt cursed. Some people had bad luck with dates, others had bad luck with cars. Andy was convinced that he had bad luck with jobs and would never find another one. There was no end in sight for his days as an Office Haven employee.

A month ago, he'd finally had a breaking point when he had to pull funds from his grocery money to get a haircut. He didn't even want to waste money on a haircut, but his manager at Office Haven told him that, according to the employee handbook, shaggy hair wasn't acceptable. Apparently, corporate cared less about their employees eating and more about them "maintaining the company's image."

It was the straw that broke the camel's back. Andy ended up as a blubbering mess on the floor of his bathroom while he stared helplessly at his banking app. Andy *never* cried for anything, and the fact that he was crying made him all the more upset.

In a fit of hysterics, Andy decided that he *would* change his circumstances one way or a-fucking-nother. He told himself with an edge of madness in his voice that he'd start doing porn. Hell, everyone else was doing it—why couldn't he?

With tears in his eyes and only partly aware of what he was doing, he went to his laptop, submitted a request to open a FanFrenzy profile, and submitted a picture of his driver's license to prove that he was over eighteen. By the time he got his approval email forty-eight hours later, his meltdown had long since ended and he'd calmed down considerably (thanks to Wyatt who had generously offered to help him out with groceries until his next paycheck). To his surprise, the idea of doing porn didn't repulse his coherent, emotionally sound mind as much as he thought it would. He'd been told by more than a few girls in the past that he was handsome, and thanks to the small gym in the apartment complex, he stayed in decent shape. Honestly, this FanFrenzy thing seemed like a real chance to make money. It was sure to pay better than Office Haven.

So, he decided to give it a shot. It was awkward at first, but ultimately not as bad as he'd expected. Honestly, cashiering at Office Haven was *far* worse than getting naked online for strangers, which should tell you how miserable his retail job was.

He'd amassed a reasonable following in a matter of weeks, and if he could keep it up and make a little bit more money per month, then he could walk into Office Haven and tell his manager the words he's been dying to tell him since he started:

I fucking QUIT!

But in the back of his mind, he thought about Wyatt. He couldn't bear to tell him the truth. If he knew what he was doing, he would completely freak out, no doubt about it. Andy was certain that if Wyatt knew the extent to what he was doing, he wouldn't want to be his friend anymore.

So, he planned to take this secret to his grave.

Chapter One

"It just came in the mail yesterday. I haven't even opened it yet. Do you guys want to see?" Andy smiled into the camera of his laptop as the group chat blew up with excitement:

Omg yes plz!!

Yasssss

I wanna see~! ;)

He laughed, "Alright, alright. I'll open it. Also, big shoutout to fandaddy58 for buying this for me off my wishlist." Fandaddy58 responded in the chat with a blushing emoji.

Andy grabbed a pair of scissors from his desk drawer and began carefully cutting the tape on the cardboard package. "I've gotta admit, I'm a little nervous. I've never used one of these before. I hope it's not too big…"

He opened the box, lifted out the brown packing paper from the top, and froze. His mouth dropped open, stunned, and a nervous laugh escaped from his throat. Curious commenters were flooding the group chat, eager to see what he was looking at. He reached in a pulled out a terrifyingly large, realistic-looking dildo.

"*This* is eight inches?!" he asked incredulously. "There's no way!"

The chat was in an uproar.

LMFAOOOO

asdfghjkl

IM DEAD RN LOL

This is how u know guys are always lying about how big 8 inches rly is xD

Andy blushed. In the past, he'd always told girls he was roughly eight inches, but according to the dimensions of the dildo in his hands, he realized that seven was probably more accurate.

"I don't know if I'm going to be able to do anything with this thing, you guys… It's fucking huge."

Three weeks ago, thanks to the persistent coaxing from his fans, Andy begrudgingly agreed to try out some mild ass play and fingered himself for the first time. It had been an eye-opening experience, to say the least. He was expecting to hate every second of it, but it was surprisingly…pleasant. Hell, it was better than pleasant—it felt *amazing*. He ended up taking three fingers by the end of the first session and had one of the best orgasms of his life.

His fans ate it up.

Word had apparently spread about the straight boy who was experimenting with butt stuff for the first time on camera because he gained almost fifty new subscribers overnight. It was at that point in his newly budding porn career that he'd decided that he was making enough money to finally leave Office Haven. He went in the following day and quit on the spot.

That had also felt amazing.

Since then, Andy had incorporated butt play into most of his live streams and his subscribers continued to grow steadily. He quickly got accustomed to posing seductively for the camera and spreading his cheeks wide for the world to see. It was new and utterly unfamiliar—he'd never considered that his butt could be one of his assets—but he found that he enjoyed the attention. Since starting his FanFrenzy account, Andy had been getting a *lot* of praise, more than he'd ever gotten in his life. *You're so sexy! Your body is perfect! You have a hot cock!* But more than anything else, compliments directed at his backside made him preen the most. Because damn it, he *did* have a nice butt, and it was high time it got the appreciation it deserved.

Truth be told, since exploring the strange and exciting world of ass play, Andy had gained a greater appreciation for his own butt, too. Who knew that sticking things in it could feel so good?

Taking fingers had been easy enough and thoroughly enjoyable—in fact, Andy found himself fingering his bum even when he was masturbating alone and the camera wasn't recording—and so, he thought it was time to get more adventurous to keep his audience engaged. A dildo felt like the next logical step.

However, the dildo he had in his hands right now felt like much more than just the next little step. It felt like swapping out a water pistol for a fucking bazooka.

"I probably should've asked for something smaller…" Andy said sheepishly.

Fandaddy58 responded with a crying emoji and dozens of other audience members quickly jumped in, laying the guilt on thick.

Aww poor fandaddy :((

I bet he's been looking forward to this all week…

Hope it wasn't expensive :/

The people pleaser part of Andy winced. He didn't know this fandaddy58 person at all, but still, he'd bought him a gift, and it hadn't been cheap—this was a high-quality dildo. Another part of Andy, the one that was terrified of losing subscribers and having to crawl back to Office

Haven, also winced. If his brief time as a Junior Account Executive had taught him anything, it was that customer happiness was the key to success. (Of course, the company Andy learned that from went bankrupt in the end, so clearly there was a *bit* more involved to success than just customer happiness. But that's beside the point.)

Someone else posted in the chat:

It probably isn't as bad as you think! It's long, but not super thick. Long and skinny is better than short and thick, believe me.

A few others responded, agreeing with the sentiment. Andy looked down at the dildo. It was true—while long, it wasn't very girthy. Perhaps his initial impression of it being "terrifyingly large" had been an exaggeration.

"Maybe you're right," he said finally. "Maybe it won't be that bad. It couldn't hurt to at least try, right?"

Poor choice of words, he thought. When it came to shoving things up one's ass, it very much *could* hurt to try. But the chat buzzed with encouragement and anticipation. Fandaddy58 responded with a smiley face and a heart emoji. There was no backing out now.

As Andy began cutting into the hard plastic packaging the dildo came in—*why did they make these damn things so hard to get into?*—he glanced up at the screen and caught a question amid the steady stream of incoming chats.

Is your roommate home?

Andy had been smart enough—or maybe deranged enough—to build his FanFrenzy presence on the gimmick that he was a straight boy secretly making porn while his other straight roommate remained clueless. While Andy had done no research into the adult entertainment market before starting his account, he'd managed to choose a pretty effective schtick. Call it beginner's luck, but the roommate-secretly-making-porn stunt definitely drew a crowd.

In the early days, he started posting pictures and videos taken with his phone of him stealthily pulling out his cock when Wyatt was nearby. Sometimes he was in the kitchen while Wyatt was on the couch in the living room, or vice versa, but on one or two occasions, Andy had managed to slip his dick out of the leg of his basketball shorts while they were on the couch together. Wyatt had been oblivious.

It was these initial pictures and videos that had put his FanFrenzy account on the map, and his fans constantly asked for more titillating content like that. Andy did something risky around Wyatt once a week at most, just enough to keep his subscribers happy. Truth be told, though, he was rather ashamed about it. He knew he was betraying Wyatt by hiding this from him and by involving him unknowingly in his porn career, but without the "sneaky roommate" gimmick, he feared his FanFrenzy success would wane and go belly up just like the tech start-up had.

"Nope," Andy answered, finally prying the dildo from the plastic. "He left for work an hour ago. He's got a proper 9-to-5."

Then, someone in the chat by the name of str8boyaddict commented:

I'll tip you $250 to use that dildo in his bed right now.

Andy's eyes went wide and he blushed furiously at the thought. "Absolutely not! There is no way I could do that to him."

The rest of the chat clearly sided with str8boyaddict.

But he'd never know!

@str8boyaddict god, your mind…

U should totally do it!! >:)

That would be sooo hot

Don't be a wuss LOL

Andy tried to laugh them off, "You guys are crazy. As if shoving this anaconda up my ass wasn't stressful enough as it is."

Then, str8boyaddict commented again.

How about $500?

Andy bit his lip and began giving this proposition some serious consideration. In the chat, there was a tidal wave of eye emojis pouring in from other users. Everyone was waiting for his answer.

Before he could even open his mouth to say anything, str8boyaddict sent another message.

$1000. Final offer.

The chat went berserk.

HOLY SHIT!

BRO. If you don't ur a damn FOOL.

Hell, I'LL jerk off on your roommate's bed for $1000 lmao

Why is this literally the most suspenseful thing i've ever seen? sksksk

"Okay, okay!" Andy said finally, his cheeks burning scarlet. That one user was right, he would be a fool not to do it. It was a thousand bucks for, like, thirty minutes of work at most. He knew Wyatt would be mortified by the truth, but he never needed to know. Besides, Andy was intending to use some of the money he'd been earning with FanFrenzy to pay Wyatt back for everything he'd done to help him through the past few months. He planned to tell him that he'd gotten a remote freelance job—which was kinda true—except that he knew Wyatt would ask questions about it. Andy wanted to make sure that his cover story was bulletproof before he told him anything because the last thing he wanted was to get caught in a lie and have the truth exposed.

"Alright," he said, wiping his suddenly sweaty palms on his basketball shorts, "If you send the tip, str8boy, I'll do it."

A moment later, a chime rang out, indicating that someone had sent him a tip. There it was—$1000, as promised. It was the largest single tip he'd ever gotten and he was simultaneously thrilled and anxious. Some part of him had hoped that str8boyaddict had just been bluffing. But now he had the money, which meant he had to uphold his end of the deal.

The chat filled with eggplant and peach emojis. *Let's get this over with*, he thought.

Andy gave the best flirtatious smile that he could manage and said, "Alright, str8boy, you're getting your wish. Thanks for the donation."

He grabbed the dildo and a small bottle of water-based lube with one hand and picked up his laptop with the other. His heart was racing as he exited his bedroom and padded across the small living room to the opposite side where Wyatt's door stood ajar. He peeked inside nervously, half expecting to see him inside. That was ridiculous, of course, because he'd heard him leave for work an hour ago.

The coast was clear, as he knew it would be, and so he pushed inside. He'd been in Wyatt's room countless times but never without him being there. This felt wrong on so many levels. He didn't even want to imagine the repercussions of getting caught in here doing what he was about to do. But there was no chance of that happening, he told himself. Wyatt wouldn't be home for another eight hours or so.

"I know that I've literally taken dick pics while sitting next to my roommate before, but this feels like the riskiest thing I've ever done," Andy laughed and looked down into the camera. "And he's not even here!"

The group chat sent him messages of encouragement. After a quick glance around, he placed his laptop on Wyatt's chest of drawers; it was almost perfectly bed-level, so it gave everyone a good view of the show.

"Whoops, I forgot a towel," he told the camera and winked. "You guys know how explosive my orgasms are when I'm playing with my ass."

After a hasty jog back to his bathroom, Andy returned with a towel and instinctively closed Wyatt's door behind him. He laid the towel out onto Wyatt's perfectly made bed and made a mental note to himself to smooth out the comforter when he was done so that Wyatt wouldn't notice he'd been there.

Then, he turned back to his computer again and asked, "Are you ready?"

OH yeah!

Yes yes yes! Pull out that hot cock, stud ;)

Fuck I'm so hard right now...

I can't believe he's really doing it, this is amazing

Well, here goes nothing. He hooked his thumbs into the waistband of his shorts, the only article of clothing he was wearing, and pushed them down easily. Despite the undercurrent of guilt and anxiety he felt to be doing this in Wyatt's room, he already had a semi.

He ran a hand down his abs and tugged slowly along the length of his cock. Like a proper porn star, he groaned and let his eyes fall closed as he stroked himself. There was a lot to this job that was purely theatrical, but even still, it didn't take much before he was fully hard. Alongside the guilt, there was also a quivering, naughty rush of adrenaline stirring inside of him that was spurring on his erection. Being in Wyatt's room felt like jerking off in public or something.

Once sufficiently hard and leaking precum, he moved back to the bed and laid down on the towel. He tried not to think about the fact that everything around him smelled like Wyatt. If he let himself think too much about his best friend, he was certain that his boner would shrink and die.

Remember that this is your job, he told himself. *You're getting paid to do this. Don't think too much about it. Just do what you came to do and leave.*

Leaning back on his elbows, he lifted his legs into the air to showcase his ass. He slid one hand down his balls until the tip of his middle finger found his entrance. He tapped it a few times teasingly and bit his lip, making eyes at the camera. His cock unintentionally jumped. He observed with mild amusement that he'd conditioned his body to expect sex whenever something got close to his hole. That sweet spot inside him that he'd discovered was already awake and hungry for stimulation. Maybe this dildo thing wouldn't be so bad after all.

He slicked up his fingers and pressed one in. The gentle moan that came out of him that time wasn't an act. Then, he slipped in a second, and a moment later, a third. A deep flush had spread across his face and chest, something that always happened when he played with his prostate. As he moved his fingers in and out, his cock twitched and leaked onto his abs.

His body was ready for more now. Not just ready—*eager* for more. He grabbed the dildo and coated it generously with lube, stroking it like he might stroke himself. The dildo was so realistic that for a moment, he could envision himself stroking someone else's actual cock. He almost laughed out loud at the idea. There was no way in *hell* he would ever touch another dude's dick. Not for all the money in str8boyaddict's bank account.

Once the dildo was good and lubed up, he guided it down between his legs and, using two clumsy hands, aligned the tip of the realistic cock head to his hole. Then, he took a few deep breaths—he read online somewhere that it was best to be as relaxed as possible when on the receiving end of anal play—and gently pushed. The tip of the dildo began to stretch him out and *holy moly Mother of God.* His first impression *had* been right. This thing was fucking huge!

His instinct was to clench, but he silently told himself not to. He took a few more breaths, trying to stay relaxed, and continued pushing it inside of him. At last, the firm ridge of the cock head made it past his tight ring of muscle, and he almost cried out in joy. The damn thing was finally inside him. Well, partially inside him anyway. And to Andy, that felt like a personal victory. He let out a sigh of relief, and immediately the muscles in his body loosened. Evidently, he'd not been as relaxed as he thought he was. Oops.

"Whichever one of you said this wouldn't be as bad as I thought it would is a fucking liar," he laughed, looking at his laptop. He was too far away to read the chat clearly but he could just make out that the window had filled with laughing emojis.

Now that it was in and his body had begun to relax around its girth, the dildo wasn't so bad anymore. Slowly, he pushed it farther in and another moan escaped his lips as the shaft dragged along his prostate. *Fuck.* That was good. *Really* good. Experimenting with his fingers had been amazing, but this was scratching a certain itch within him that his fingers never could. He totally understood why pegging was a thing now.

He pushed it in further still and his hips unconsciously rolled against it.

"*God,*" he breathed. His head fell back against the mattress as he began working the thing in and out of himself slowly. With each pass, he drove the dildo deeper and deeper inside. Finally, to his surprise, it bottomed out. He had all eight inches of realistic cyberskin cock in his ass.

"Well, that went better than expected," he said to the camera and chuckled. "Thanks again, fandaddy58. This thing is incredible."

His eyes fluttered shut, and he began steadily fucking himself with the dildo. His cock was painfully tight, bouncing with every deep plunge. A string of low moans floated through the air as he lost himself in the pleasure of his sweet spot and the heat of his building orgasm. He was only vaguely aware that he shouldn't allow himself to come too quickly, but he couldn't remember the reason. He'd forgotten all about the camera and the audience watching him on the other side of the screen.

"*Fuck*," he groaned. His orgasm was rapidly approaching and he wasn't even touching his cock. That was new. He'd heard of guys having hands-free orgasms before, but that was never something he'd even gotten close to doing before. But at this rate, he was certain he was going to come whether he touched himself or not.

Andy was too blissed out to hear the front door closing. Nor did he hear someone cautiously call his name from elsewhere in the apartment or the sound of Wyatt's door being opened. But he *did* hear the shocked and horrified voice yelling only a few feet away.

"*DUDE, WHAT THE FUCK!?*"

Chapter Two

Wyatt slid into the driver's seat of his beat-up sedan and let out a sigh. His dental appointment had gone well—no cavities, thank goodness—but now it was time to head into work. Most people he knew hated the dentist, but Wyatt had been hoping that the appointment would've lasted longer than it did. He'd rather get a root canal than go back into the office.

He would've taken the entire day off from work except that the company offered minimal PTO days. It wasn't smart to waste a whole day on something as mundane as a dentist appointment. As it was, he'd already missed four days back in February thanks to a bad cold and one day in May because of a flat tire he'd gotten on his morning commute. If he missed much more, he wouldn't have enough time left over to take a week off around Christmas to see his family.

He looked at his reflection in the rearview mirror for a moment. His eyes looked tired and dull. He wasn't sure how much longer he could keep trudging through the weeks like this. Sometimes on his lunch break, he skimmed through local job listings, but nothing he saw excited him. Even if his job as a Payroll Specialist was easier at another company, it would still be a drag. Spending the rest of his life hunched over a computer, triple-checking spreadsheets every single day, didn't sound appealing.

It was like he'd told Andy a couple of months back, his life already felt over at the tender age of twenty-three.

Sighing again, he drew his seatbelt over his chest, and as he clicked it into place, he noticed that his building badge wasn't clipped to his belt loop like it normally was. Shit, he must've left it on his other khakis this morning. He was probably too concerned with making it to his dentist appointment on time.

Oh well. So what if he had to make a fifteen-minute detour back home before going into the office? It wasn't like Sue Ellen would know. And maybe, just for fun, he'd take the long route on his way to work. By that time, it would be close to lunchtime, and once lunch was over, he was halfway through his shift. He perked up a little at the thought.

He drove across town back to his apartment at a leisurely pace. Then, after finding a spot in the parking garage, he took the elevator up to the fourth and top floor of the building. As he fished his house key out of his pocket, he wondered absently if Andy was home. He'd told him that he had a shift at Office Haven today, but he couldn't remember when he said it started.

Stepping into the kitchen, Wyatt heard a low, muffled voice from somewhere in the apartment. He thought for a second that Andy was on the phone, except that Andy's bedroom door was wide open and it seemed to be empty. Upon listening more closely, it was apparent that the sound was coming from *his* room. That was weird.

He closed the front door behind him and ventured in cautiously, "Andy?"

There was no response, but the muffled noises continued. He approached his bedroom and was surprised to find his door closed; he was sure he'd left it open. Something was definitely off, and it made him uneasy.

He pressed his ear lightly against the door and listened. The sounds were a bit clearer, but they didn't make any sense. They sounded like…

Nope. No way.

That *couldn't* be what he was hearing. Yes, it was odd that Andy was apparently in his room with the door closed. And yes, the noises he heard sounded…obscene. But there had to be some kind of logical explanation.

There was only one way to solve the mystery. He turned the knob and pushed the door open.

The sight awaiting him on the other side froze him in his tracks. He couldn't process *what* he was actually looking at. It was like his brain had short-circuited and completely shut off.

It was Andy, on his bed, legs in the air, repeatedly shoving a rather large dildo into his ass. His head was thrown back on the bed; a deep flush was splashed across his face and chest. He was moaning and moving his hips in rhythm with the dildo.

I'm dreaming right now, Wyatt thought absently. *Yeah, this is just a dream. A nightmare more like it.*

Then, he was violently brought back to reality as Andy's panting became more erratic and he began reaching for his erection with his free hand. Wyatt realized all at once that A) this wasn't a dream, B) Andy—his best friend—was, in fact, jerking off on his bed while he was home alone, and C) he was about to watch him come.

Wyatt's brain was back online again and suddenly he could move. He opened his mouth and yelled the only thing that he could think to say.

"DUDE, WHAT THE FUCK!?"

A lot of things happened next.

Andy screamed—not just a little shout of surprise, but *screamed*—and sat up as fast as he could, letting go of the dildo in the process. As a result, it launched out of his ass with an audible *pop!* and fell to the carpet. Then, Andy scrambled off the bed, yelling out a string of panicked expletives at the top of his lungs, and slammed his laptop shut, which Wyatt had only just noticed was there. All the while, Andy's rapidly shrinking hard-on was swinging around wildly with a slick thread of precum dangling from the tip and threatening to stick to the first thing it touched.

It was like witnessing a train wreck—Wyatt couldn't tear his eyes away from the disaster unfolding before him.

Once the laptop was closed, Andy frantically grabbed the towel from the bed and covered his crotch with it. He started at Wyatt with wide-eyed terror.

"I-I can explain!" he yelped.

All of sudden, Wyatt's emotions caught up with him, and boy were there a lot of them. Shock, embarrassment, confusion, betrayal, disgust, and anger swirled around inside his head and heart.

In the end, his anger was the loudest of the bunch, and he let it fill him up completely. Squaring his shoulders and balling his hands into tight fists, he turned on his heel and marched out into the living room without a word, slamming the door hard behind him. He began pacing, unsure what else to do. On the one hand, he was beyond upset right now and didn't want to be near Andy, but also, he wanted answers.

About half a minute later, his bedroom door creaked open tentatively and Andy stepped out, wearing basketball shorts. He'd covered his upper body by wrapping the towel around his shoulders. His face was an unappealing gray color; he looked like he was about to be sick. But Wyatt couldn't muster any sympathy for him. He folded his strong arms over his chest and looked away.

"I am so, so sorry, Wyatt," Andy said quietly, taking a small step into the living room. "There's no excuse for what I did, but I need you to know that I didn't *want* to do it, okay?"

Wyatt whipped his head around to look at him, face full of incredulity. "What the hell do you mean you *didn't want* to do it!? No one was in there forcing you to jerk off on my bed, Andy! If you don't want to do something, you just don't fucking do it! It's that simple!" He puffed out an exasperated breath and ran his hands through his hair, "How long has this been going on?"

"Just today!" Andy said hastily. "I swear it. And it was only supposed to be a one-time th—"

Wyatt cut him off. "I just can't believe you would actually do something like that. I thought we were friends, dude."

"We are friends! And I really am sorry! I can't apologize enough. But it's really not what you think—"

Wyatt, who was barely listening to anything coming out of Andy's mouth suddenly remembered the dildo he'd been using. Had Andy been imagining that *he* was fucking him? The idea made him blush with embarrassment.

"Are you gay?" he asked bluntly.

43

Andy blinked, surprised. "What? No, I'm not gay!"

"Because it's okay if you are!" Wyatt added quickly, sweat breaking on his forehead. All at once, he felt completely out of his depth. "I don't have anything against gay people at all. I-I actually have a cousin who's gay. He's a super cool dude—uh, guy. So, don't feel like you can't tell me if you are. It's just that, I don't feel that, um, way about you...like that. I'm super flattered that you feel that way about me, though. But, um, it's also not cool to do something like that in someone's bed. I'm not trying to be close-minded or anything! I just think—"

"I'm not gay!" Andy said again, impatiently. "I had three girlfriends in college!"

"Oh, shit, right. Sorry. I mean bisexual."

"I'm not that either!" he huffed. "I'm just making porn!"

Wyatt stared at him and blinked several times. "...What?"

Andy sighed and looked down at the ground. "I've been meaning to tell you that I got a new job recently, but I wasn't sure how to do it. The cat is definitely out of the bag now though," he let out a humorless laugh. "For the past two and a half months, I've been working as a cam model on FanFrenzy. And the only reason I was in your bed doing...*stuff* was because some guy paid me a thousand bucks to do it."

This news came as both a shock and a relief to Wyatt. While he was still pissed at the complete violation of his privacy and personal space, this situation was a bit easier to grapple with than the idea that Andy had been harboring an unhealthy crush on him all this time. Nevertheless, the truth was still absolutely mind-boggling. Andy doing *porn*? Wyatt had so many questions.

"Dude, *why* are you even cam modeling in the first place?"

"Jesus, Wyatt, why do you think? Because I'm fucking desperate!" he retorted. "I've been running around like a headless chicken for *months* trying to find a goddamn job, and I got sick and tired of barely making ends meet, living paycheck to paycheck. I was tired of getting rejection emails from jobs I applied to and worrying about money all the fucking time. So, I took matters into my own hands."

"Andy, I know things have been rough, but *porn*? How can do stuff like that," he waved a hand toward his bedroom, "and let other people watch? It doesn't feel...*dirty* to you?

"At first, yeah," he admitted. "But then I realized that it's just a job like anything else. I provide a service that other people pay to see. That's it."

"But you're selling your body…"

"*So*?!" he said hotly. "How is that any different than spending forty hours a week, every week for the rest of your life at some stupid office job? People waste their entire lives working for some company that couldn't give a shit if they live or die."

Wyatt clamped his mouth shut and swallowed. Andy was right. He was saying everything that Wyatt himself had been thinking about for months but never put into words. Except, what did it matter if he put it into words or not? It wouldn't change the facts—this was just the way the world fucking worked. Nobody *liked* having a job, but everyone had to have one to pay the bills and put food on the table. And there was no way that doing porn was somehow the more empowering and liberating option when you had to literally shake your junk for strangers on the internet. A traditional, soul-sucking 9-to-5 was better than *that*, surely.

Wyatt shrugged, "Well, if you're fine with doing that sort of thing, I guess that's all that matters…" He just remembered something Andy had said before. "Wait. Did you say that one single person paid you *a thousand* dollars to jerk off on my bed?"

"Yeah. Turns out people are really into the 'naughty roommate' thing."

"Jesus... Do they always pay that much?"

"No, not normally, but tips don't make up the bulk of my income anyway. My subscribers pay ten dollars a month to access my channel. Tips are just the icing on the cake."

"So, how many subscribers do you have?"

"Last I checked, I was at seven hundred and forty-three."

Wyatt gawked at him. "You're making over *seven thousand* dollars a month doing this?"

"Well, the site takes a twenty percent cut, but after tips, it's roughly seven thousand, yeah."

"That's eighty-four thousand dollars a year!" He couldn't believe what he was hearing. That was more than he made. A good deal more.

"Dude, that's what I'm saying! For the first time in months, I'm not constantly stressing out! I'm actually making payments toward my student loans again, and I've been putting money into my savings, too."

Something in Wyatt softened. Hearing that Andy was finally able to start chipping away at the mountain of student debt that's been haunting him for months genuinely made him happy. In a weird way, he felt a sense of secondhand relief. Wyatt had understood that Andy's financial struggles posed a threat to both of their lives. If things got bad enough, Andy might've had to go back home to live with his parents, and Wyatt didn't want that—not only for Andy's sake but his own as well. He didn't have any other close friends in the city; he'd be all alone. On top of that, he didn't want to have to find a new roommate. Not only was the process a headache, but Wyatt wholeheartedly enjoyed Andy's company. They lived together well, and he was his best friend for crying out loud. He didn't want to lose him.

Now, for the first time in ages, Wyatt also stopped stressing about Andy's finances. He had to admit, it felt good.

"Also," Andy continued, "I've been saving up to give you a little surprise, too. I'm going to cover the next two months of rent for both of us."

Wyatt was taken aback. "Really? Why?"

Andy shrugged, "Because I can afford to do it. And more than that, I just wanted to thank you for all of your help lately." He chuckled, "I probably would've starved to death without you."

"Well, geez... That's really nice of you to offer, but you don't have to do that. If you wanna cover my groceries one week or something, that's fine, but two months' worth of rent is a lot of money."

"I know, but it's not just about the groceries." Andy let out a sigh and rubbed the back of his neck, "I just want to do something nice for you. I know how much you hate your job and I can't help but feel like it's partially my fault you're in that hellhole. You wouldn't have come to this city to begin with if it wasn't for me."

Wyatt's eyes went wide. "You don't really think that way, do you? Andy, listen to me. You're in no way responsible for my shitty job, okay? I chose to come to this city with you, I chose to apply to this company, and above all else, I chose to accept their job offer. None of that is your fault."

"I guess, but I still can't help but feel partly responsible. Also, I feel bad that we haven't gone out and done anything fun in ages because my broke ass couldn't afford to do anything. And you never once complained! You just stayed at home on the weekends and kept me company. I can't even begin to tell you how much I appreciate that, dude. So, will you please just let me do this nice thing for you?"

Andy watched him with nervous anticipation. Wyatt wanted to refuse—as generous as the otter was, he didn't like being on the receiving end of extravagant gifts. But he knew Andy really wanted to do this for him. He could see it in his earnest hazel eyes. Maybe accepting the gift was more for Andy's benefit than his own, and maybe that was okay. He didn't want him feeling responsible for his own shitty circumstances. If covering two months of rent would help him feel absolved of his misplaced guilt, then Wyatt would allow it. Besides, not having to think about rent for a couple of months sounded nice.

The corner of Wyatt's mouth quirked into a small smile, "If you *really* want to pay for my rent, I don't suppose I can stop you."

Andy's shoulders visibly relaxed, and he smiled. "I'll take that as a yes. Thanks, man."

"I feel like I should be thanking you in this situation," Wyatt laughed. The heavy tension that had filled the room suddenly felt lighter.

"So," Andy started shyly. "Are we going to be okay?"

When Wyatt had stormed out after finding Andy in his bed, he didn't imagine that he would ever be able to look him in the eye again. He'd been in no mood to mend bridges at the time anyway, but even if he had been, he didn't have a clue how friends could possibly recover from something like *that*. Yet, here they were. Talking and laughing just like always.

Part of Wyatt was still upset, of course. Not only because Andy had kept this porn thing a secret from him for so long, but also because he caught him using a goddamn dildo in his goddamn bed. But, to his surprise, that felt like something he'd get over with time, something that they'd end up looking back on and laughing about someday. More than anything, Wyatt was just glad to see Andy doing well for a change. He had noticed a subtle shift in his stress levels lately but couldn't figure out what was different. Now it all made sense. Andy wasn't desperate for money anymore. And he finally seemed more like his old self again—buoyant and optimistic.

So what if he was making ends meet with porn? Wyatt couldn't blame him.

"Yeah," he said finally, giving him a smile. "We're okay, Andrew."

51

Andy's face broke out into a brilliant grin; the relief was evident throughout his entire body. "You're the best, man."

"However," Wyatt added sternly, "you have to promise me that you'll never film porn in my bed again."

Andy raised one hand and crossed his heart with the other, "I promise. Scout's honor."

"And you gonna clean the lube off of my carpet."

"Was already planning on it. I'm going to wash your bedding, too."

"Good," Wyatt nodded, satisfied. "It's going to take some time to get used to this whole cam model thing, but I think I can make my peace with it." A thought crossed his mind then that stirred up a few butterflies of anxiety in his gut. "Aren't you afraid someone you know will find out, though?"

"Yeah. *You.*"

"Oh, right… Fair enough. But what about other friends? Or your family?"

Andy shrugged, "Not really. I don't think there's much overlap between my social circle and my FanFrenzy audience. Most of my subscribers are gay men."

Wyatt thought about this and then asked, "You're not using your real name are you?"

"Of course not, dude. Give me a little credit here," Andy said with a good-natured eyeroll. "I go by the name Ace."

"Ace?" he teased.

"What's wrong with Ace? It's a sexy name!"

"Must be if you've already gotten seven hundred subscribers," he grinned. Then, he glanced at the clock on the wall. "Shit, I've got to get to work. But we'll talk more about this later, Ace."

Andy groaned. "I'm never going to live this down am I?"

"Not a chance."

Chapter Three

After Wyatt left, Andy returned to the scene of the crime, and he was suddenly reliving the traumatic ordeal of having been walked in on by his best friend with an eight-inch dildo in his ass. Things between him and Wyatt seemed fairly okay after their talk, but remembering the look of horror on his face when he caught him in the act made Andy want to curl up in a ball and die. He was sure that Wyatt would be haunted by that mental image for the rest of his life. Coincidentally, the experience would haunt Andy, too.

He tried to shake the feelings of embarrassment from his head and began cleaning up the shameful mess he'd left behind. When he picked up the dildo from the ground, it was covered in random little hairs and flecks of dirt.

"Gross…"

He took it to his bathroom and washed it thoroughly before returning to Wyatt's room. The lube on the carpet washed out easily—thank God for water-based lube. Then he stripped the bed and put the bedding in the washing machine.

Once the evidence was gone, Andy expected to feel a little bit better about everything, but he had no such luck. He couldn't shake the feelings of guilt within him. In their five years of friendship, he and Wyatt had never once had an argument, but he'd single-handedly ruined their perfect track record today. The friction between them felt like an ugly ink blot on the previously immaculate canvas of their relationship. Andy wanted more than anything to scrub the stain away, but the ink had already absorbed into the fabric. The damage had been done. Of course, that didn't mean that they weren't still best bros. But their friendship had been forever changed today and Andy was to blame for that.

Amid the mess of icky feelings weighing on him, there were also concerns about his porn career. Andy was too ashamed to admit that he was thinking about something like that at a time like this, but some tiny part of him was. Now that Wyatt knew about his FanFrenzy account—and everyone who had been watching his live stream witnessed the revelation—the whole *my-roommate-is-clueless-about-the-porn-I-make* schtick wasn't going to fly. Andy knew that if he kept up the usual routine of taking stealthy dick pics around Wyatt (which he didn't think he could bring himself to do at this point anyway) that his subscribers would now question how authentic it was. They'd likely accuse Wyatt of being in on the charade and maybe even assume that he had been all along. Andy's FanFrenzy popularity was sure to take a nosedive.

He scrubbed a hand over his face and then ran it through his tousled brown hair. This was too much for his brain to process all at once. He needed to get out of the house.

The clock informed him that his personal training session at the gym wouldn't start for another forty-five minutes, but he decided that getting there early and spending half an hour on the treadmill may help to clear his head. So, he got up and changed into his workout clothes.

The fancy gym that he'd signed up with the month before, Fitness 365, was only two blocks away from their apartment, so he walked. At this time of day, it wasn't crowded at all and he found a machine in the corner of the room facing the window. After a light warm-up, he set the treadmill at a brisk speed and let the steady rhythm of his footsteps drown out his worries.

Before he knew it, someone was tapping on his arm and pulling him out of his flow. He stopped the treadmill.

"You're here early," said a voice. He turned to find Leslie, his personal trainer, staring back at him with a slightly amused look on her face.

Andy looked around and blinked as if dazed. "Is it time already?"

"That's what my watch says," she said dryly. "I hope you didn't tire yourself out on that thing. I've got a brutal workout planned for you today."

"Great." He tried to laugh but it sounded thin to his own ears. Since he'd stopped running, his worries were all rushing back to him. "I'm ready when you are." The sooner he got out of his head, the better.

Andy took a long sip from his water bottle as he followed Leslie to the weight room. When he started making real money with FanFrenzy, he decided that he had to keep his body in tip-top shape and that the dinky little gym at the apartment complex wouldn't suffice. So, he signed up at

Fitness 365 and hired a trainer to meet with him Monday through Friday. He'd specifically chosen Leslie based solely on her profile picture on the gym's website. She was around his age, blonde, and very cute. In person, Andy discovered that she was five-foot-one, just as cute as her picture, and a total drill sergeant. During his first week of training with her, he actually had to cancel one of his FanFrenzy live streams because his arms were so sore following one of her workouts that he couldn't even jerk off.

After a few weeks of torture, she eased up on him a bit and became a good deal friendlier. Andy felt as though he had passed some sort of test. He reasoned that she probably put all of her dude-bro clients through a rigorous trial period to knock them down a few pegs and show them who was boss. It worked. Andy respected and feared her far too much to even think about flirting with her.

Today's workout was focused on chest and arms. Leslie guided him through a variety of different exercises using free weights, resistance bands, and weight machines. He took to the exercises with a greater sense of focus and concentration than usual. Just as the treadmill had helped, so too did Leslie's workout regime. He was working up a nice sweat and his troubles felt far away again.

About forty minutes into the workout, though, he was brought back to reality when Leslie tossed a fresh towel in his face and asked, "What's with you today?"

"Huh?" he asked, using the towel to wipe his brow. "What do you mean?"

"You're quiet today. Normally I can't get you to shut up. Also, you're not checking out my butt every five seconds like you usually do."

Andy turned red. He hadn't realized she'd noticed that. But of course she did. Leslie had the eyes of a hawk. She could spot bad form from a mile away.

"Sorry," he said shyly. "I won't do it anymore."

She rolled her eyes. "I don't care about that. I know I have a nice butt—it's fine. I'm more bothered about what's gotten into you."

Beneath her look of mild impatience was a glimpse of real concern.

"It's nothing," he mumbled. "Just had an argument with my roommate is all. It's no big deal."

"Oh yeah? Well, what happened?"

She was giving him her full attention. Shit. He was hoping they'd just move on from the subject, but apparently not.

He tried being vague. "Eh, nothing really. He just got a little mad that I didn't tell him about my new job. That's all."

She frowned. "Why would your roommate care about your job?"

"Well, he's my best friend. We usually share that sort of stuff."

Her frown deepened. "Well, if he's your best friend, why didn't you just tell him about your new job?

Andy was starting to feel flustered. "Why am I being interrogated right now?"

"Because what you're saying isn't making any sense," she said bluntly. "Why would you keep your job a secret from your best friend? That's dumb."

"Not when your new job is—" He bit his tongue.

"Not when your new job is what?"

God, she was relentless, and her small reserves of patience were clearly running thin. He was going to end up in a second argument today if he wasn't careful, and he was still recovering from the first.

He sighed and buried his face in the towel. "*Prrrn*," he mumbled into the fabric.

Leslie leaned in closer, "What was that?"

Lifting his head, he whispered sharply, "*Porn!*"

Her eyebrows shot up and her mouth dropped open. Curiosity and amusement twinkled in her eyes. "Are you *serious*?"

Burying his face back into the towel, Andy gave a small, pathetic nod. He couldn't remember the last time he'd had such a thoroughly embarrassing day.

"Wow," she said, shaking her head in disbelief, "I never would've guessed, honestly. That's wild." Then, after a moment, she added, "I guess that explains why you're here at noon on a Thursday then, huh? You obviously don't have a 9-to5."

He shot her an annoyed glance overtop the towel.

"How long have you been doing it?" she asked.

"Two and a half months."

She folded her arms and seemed to consider this. The initial shock had worn off quickly which Andy was quietly grateful for. Not much seemed to faze her.

"So, on the one hand, I understand why you didn't want to tell him about it," she said. "But on the other hand, if he really is your best friend, then you should've probably told him."

"Well, he *is* really my best friend."

"Then, yeah, I'd say you fucked up in this situation."

"Gee, thanks…"

She shrugged easily. "Everyone fucks up. All we can do is apologize and try to be better. In your case, you've gotta be honest with him going forward. Otherwise, you'll never regain his trust. No more secrets."

She made it sound so simple and easy. Although, maybe it *was* just that simple and easy. Granted, she didn't know the whole story—things were a bit more complicated than he'd let on, of course—but her philosophy still seemed applicable. He had to put in the work to rebuild Wyatt's trust. So, going forward, no more secrets.

"You're right," he said and gave her a small smile. "Thanks for listening."

Andy's problems hadn't magically gone away—it would take time to completely smooth things over with Wyatt, and the fate of his porn career still hung in the balance—but for a brief moment, he felt better.

"No prob," she said, returning a smile of her own. For a second, Andy thought, they felt like real friends. Then, she clapped her hands together and said, "Alright, break time's over. Hit the deck, Porn Star, and give me thirty diamond pushups."

———

Back home, showered, and completely exhausted, Andy slumped onto his bed and took a deep breath before opening his laptop. He was reluctant to assess the damage that had been done after this morning's show, but he knew he couldn't put it off forever. *Let's get this over with*, he thought.

He opened his computer and logged back into his FanFrenzy account. When the page loaded, his heart skipped a beat. There were *hundreds* of new notifications. His inbox was full of countless direct messages from curious fans.

Omg what happened!? Are you okay!?

YOOOO that genuinely gave ME a heart attack!! xD

Holy shit I can't believe you just got caught! I could tell by the look on your face that shit was NOT scripted lol

Did your roommate seriously walk in on you!?!?

Your screams will haunt me for the rest of my life lmao

R.I.P.!!!

I'm sorry but the dildo shooting out of your ass was the funniest damn thing I've ever seen in my lifeeeee sksksks

The more recent messages took on a slightly more sympathetic tone.

Are you okay? It's been a while since your broadcast...

Hey, you good??

Don't leave us hanging!!!

Bro, are you dead? lol

He closed out the messages and clicked on the notifications tab at the top of the page. Upon reading the top message, he nearly choked on his tongue.

You have 3318 new subscribers!

This had to be a mistake. There was no way this was his account. He wondered with some horror if he'd accidentally logged into someone else's account somehow, but a glance at the top right-hand corner of the page showed his profile picture and username. It was no mistake. This was really happening. But how?

He navigated to his profile page and saw that the recording from his earlier live stream had been posted to his timeline. This was a default function and one that Andy had completely forgotten about when he slammed his laptop earlier in the midst of his panic. It seemed that the broadcast had somehow gone viral since it ended. The most likely explanation was that someone had shared the video via social media and it had taken off. Now, thousands of people were invested and curious to see how things unfolded from here. The sheer volume of likes and comments on the video was astounding. It was substantially higher than anything else he'd ever posted before. There was also an *additional* three thousand dollars in tips on the video, donated by dozens of users.

Andy's heart began to race as he clicked into the Finance Report tab to see his monthly earnings. With his new grand total of four thousand and sixty-one subscribers, he'd made $32,488 after FanFrenzy fees. Adding in all of his tips, he was just over $37,000.

His mouth went dry.

$37,000. *In a single month.*

"Holy shit," he mumbled to himself. There was a sound of panic and hysteria rising in his voice, "Holy shit, holy shit, holy shit. Holy fucking *shit.*"

This was it—this was the make-it-or-break-it moment for his new career. He had to keep everyone's attention somehow; otherwise, this would all slip through his fingers. If he could keep his audience interested and engaged, there was no telling how successful his FanFrenzy page might become. But *how*?

He couldn't keep up the same gimmick as before; he knew that. He had to move the story forward. His roommate had caught him in the act of filming porn *in his bed*. There was no way to casually sweep that under the rug and continue doing things as usual. So, what would the viewers want to see?

He bit his lip.

He knew the answer to that. They would want to see Wyatt. But that was ridiculous. There was no way in hell that it would ever happen, so what was the point in even thinking about it?

Still, Andy couldn't help but entertain the idea. If he could somehow convince Wyatt to join him on camera, they might end up breaking the internet. Well, probably not the *whole* internet, but maybe FanFrenzy anyway. At the very least, they were sure to draw an even bigger crowd and pull in more money.

But, no—this was nothing more than a wishful daydream. Wyatt was much shyer than Andy was, and he had been appalled at Andy's decision to do porn in the first place. The idea of him getting naked on camera was almost laughable. Andy imagined that if he asked him to join his FanFrenzy adventures, Wyatt might actually blow a fuse.

But then, what were his other options? There was nothing else that he could think of that would appeal to his followers in the same way. All of his other ideas were subpar at best and bound to disappoint. This was the only thing that was almost guaranteed to satisfy the fans' hunger.

Two straight roommates getting on camera and jerking off together? It was a recipe for success, he was sure of it.

If only Wyatt would agree.

Andy fell back onto his pillows and let out a frustrated sigh. He was on the brink of something life-changing. He could feel it. Unfortunately, the missing piece to the puzzle would never go along with it, and he would end up back at Office Haven, applying to better jobs on his fifteen-minute break, and having to decide between getting a haircut or getting groceries. The idea made him want to cry again.

He couldn't go back to Office Haven. He'd been absolutely miserable. Wyatt had seen it, too. Hell, Wyatt knew exactly what it was like to be stuck in a soul-sucking job with no end in sight...

A light bulb went off in Andy's head.

Maybe the idea of Wyatt going along with his plan wasn't so far-fetched after all. He also hated his job and might jump at the chance to make substantially more money to free himself from the 9-to-5 grind. Andy planned to split the profits fifty-fifty with him, and considering that his annual salary with four-thousand-plus subscribers was somewhere in the ballpark of $400,000, Wyatt could pull in four times his normal income in a single year. He would be able to quit his shitty job and finally be a free man.

Andy wondered, *Am I being selfish?* On some level, yes. Of course he wanted this FanFrenzy thing to work out because he didn't want to suffer through retail again. But he wasn't completely motivated by selfish reasons. Truthfully, he really did want Wyatt to be happy, too. Andy saw the spark in his eyes getting duller and duller with each passing month, and it worried him. He wanted things to go back to how they were in their college days—full of fun and optimism and happy memories. And, for the first time since graduating, he finally felt like they had a chance of getting that back.

FanFrenzy was their golden ticket.

He had to talk with him about this. Even if Wyatt ultimately said no, he had to at least try. It was like Leslie had told him: No more secrets. If this was something he was seriously considering, then Wyatt had a right to know the truth.

But if he was going to do this right, then he needed a good sales pitch. Andy opened up a blank spreadsheet and began crunching numbers. If this couldn't convince Wyatt, then nothing would.

As he fumbled his way through spreadsheet formulas and mapped out hypotheticals, he received a new direct message notification from FanFrenzy. Someone else had reached out asking him if he was okay after the stream earlier. Andy realized then that he'd left his entire fan base hanging. So, he created a new text post for his timeline and typed up an update, something just vague enough to assure people that he was alive while still keeping them guessing about what was coming next.

Hey guys. I'm alive, but everything's been turned upside down. Not sure exactly how things are going to play out. Will keep you posted. Thank you for your love and support. - Ace

Andy published the post and hoped silently to himself that the next update he'd send would be an exciting one. Wyatt, who held the fate of his porn career in his hands, would be home in a few hours and would decide how things unfolded from here.

The dryer chimed and Andy set his laptop aside to make Wyatt's bed.

Chapter Four

Wyatt spent his lunch break alone in his car on the third floor of the company parking deck. He wasn't hungry. The shock of walking in on Andy in his bed was still fresh in his mind and spoiled his appetite. He was struggling to wrap his head around the fact that his best friend would do something like that. Of course, he'd been paid a thousand bucks to do it, and Wyatt wondered if he might do the same thing for a similar price. He wasn't convinced that he would.

Andy had told him that he hadn't done anything like that before, and Wyatt desperately wanted to believe him. But he had his doubts. If he hadn't caught him in the act, would Andy have ever confessed? If there had been other instances, what incentive was there for him to tell the truth? These questions weighed on him and stung like salt on a fresh wound. Though he and Andy had ended things on a relatively positive note, the feeling of betrayal still lingered.

He wondered what other stunts Andy may have pulled over the past two and a half months for the sake of his *fans*. Curiosity ate at Wyatt until he couldn't stand it any longer. He pulled out his phone, went to the FanFrenzy site, and created a profile. He used a discreet username, of course, so Andy wouldn't find out.

It didn't take Wyatt long to find a profile run by a man named "Ace" whose bio read: *My hot, straight roommate doesn't know I make porn! ;)*

Jesus, even the bio made Wyatt blush. *Hot, straight roommate?* Andy had been adamant earlier that he was straight, but would a straight person call their best friend hot? Maybe it was all just part of the act... Yeah, that was probably it. Even still, the fact that Andy had written that about him was surreal.

Before subscribing to Andy's page and punching in his credit card details, Wyatt asked himself, *Do I really want to do this?* He'd already seen more of Andy today than he ever wanted to see in his life, and he was certain he was going to see a lot more behind the paywall. While the idea didn't thrill him, he knew he would always have questions about the truth if he didn't see it for himself. So, he paid for a month's worth of access to his page.

At the top of the page was Andy's most recent live stream, the one that Wyatt had ruined. The thumbnail showed Andy on his back with his legs in the air. The Play button had fortunately covered most of the obscene stuff.

Wyatt was surprised to see that the recording had been posted to his page at all. It didn't seem like something Andy would choose to post, but then again, what did he know? Maybe this was exactly the sort of scandalous thing the patrons of FanFrenzy wanted to see. Either way, Wyatt didn't dare click on it. He didn't care to relive the experience.

Scrolling down, he saw that Andy was posting videos and pictures every couple of days. Mostly, he appeared to be in his room, but there were a few that were taken in the kitchen and living room. Then, Wyatt came across a picture of Andy sitting on the couch with his hard cock sticking out of the leg of his basketball shorts, leaning against his thigh. In the background, sitting only a foot or two away, Wyatt saw himself on the couch facing the offscreen television, presumably playing some video game. Andy had done him the courtesy of blurring out his face, but it was undeniably him.

Wyatt gaped at the picture. Andy had taken a dick pic when he was sitting on the same couch with him!? Suddenly, he was angry all over again. Maybe Andy hadn't jerked off on his bed before today, but surely something like this was just as bad!

The image caption read: *He had no idea! ;P*

Wyatt scrolled down and saw that the thumbnail for the next video showed the kitchen. He clicked on it and watched with shock as Andy filmed himself at the kitchen sink pretending to wash dishes. Sounds of a movie played in the background. He backed away from the countertop a bit so that his lower body was in the frame and then slid his shorts down over his ass, angling it toward the camera. All the while, he looked anxiously off-screen in the direction of the living room. Their kitchen and living room had an open floor plan and were divided by a bartop.

Then, Andy pulled his shorts up, picked up his phone, and gave the audience a wink before switching to the back-facing camera and showing Wyatt on the couch in the next room, face blurred again, but clearly watching television.

Wyatt scrolled down further until he found another video set in the kitchen. He played that one, too. This was played out similarly—Andy was in the kitchen pretending to do dishes again and then stepped back so that he was in view for the camera. This time, he pulled his hard cock out from his shorts and began stroking himself. Wyatt stared in disbelief. He really had no fucking clue this has been going on. He felt like an idiot, or at the very least amazingly unobservant. How had he missed this?

The video continued with Andy gradually stroking himself faster, and then his face changed. He was wearing an expression that Wyatt recognized. It was the same one that he had earlier today in Wyatt's bed when he was approaching his orgasm. Sure enough, a few strokes later, Andy's brows pinched together and his mouth silently fell open as ropes of cum erupted forward and fell out of frame. Wyatt could he the faint sound of the load splattering onto the kitchen mat in front of the sink.

Andy's face broke out into a lazy, content grin, and he quickly wrapped his lips around his forefinger just before a small string of cum dripped off of it. Then, he winked at the camera again and turned it around to show Wyatt chilling on the couch, playing a round of *Street Kombat 7* judging by the sound effects.

When the video ended, Wyatt locked his phone and stuff it back into his khakis. His face was deeply flushed and burning hot. He could barely believe what he'd seen. Never mind the fact that he'd just witnessed his best friend blow a load *in their fucking kitchen*, he was more upset that he'd done it only one room away! This had been going on for months and Wyatt hadn't had a clue. He'd never felt so stupid in his whole life. It felt like this entire thing was some kind of weird, sick joke being played on him. Worst of all, he knew in the back of his mind that Andy was getting paid to stay at home and jerk off. And he was making *good* money, too. In fact, he was making more than Wyatt was, working forty hours a week at this stupid fucking job. Speaking of which…

The digital clock in his car said that he had five minutes left of his lunch break. So, he got out and began the walk back to the office, still fuming quietly to himself. When he made it inside, he was immediately greeted by the ruddy round face of Sue Ellen.

"Where were *you*?" she snapped, nostrils flaring and toe tapping impatiently.

Wyatt opened his mouth and closed it several times, surprised and confused. "At lunch?"

"What do you mean, *at lunch*?" she asked, putting air quotes around her words. "All morning long, our team has been here working hard to pick up the slack in *your* absence. But you decide to waltz in here half an hour before noon and then take a lunch with everyone else like you've been working hard all this time? That's shameful. A real team player wouldn't do something like that. A real team player would be at his desk, busting his butt trying to make up for the inconvenience he caused."

Wyatt's mind cycled through confusion, indignation, guilt, and fear. He was almost certain that he was entitled to his lunch hour no matter what, but he didn't know the employee handbook well enough to argue with her. Also, nobody in HR would side with him over Sue Ellen in the event of a dispute. Everyone was too afraid of her.

Unsure what else to do, he tried to appeal to her nonexistent sense of sympathy.

"But I hadn't had lunch yet," he said weakly.

She shook her head at him in disbelief, "You took all morning off! You didn't think to eat before you came in?"

"I-I couldn't eat after my dentist appointment because of the fluoride…"

She closed her eyes and let out a long, irritated sigh through her nose. "Wow, you just have a story for everything don't you, Wyatt? You'll bend over backward coming up with excuses before admitting that you were wrong about something. Isn't that right? You know, I have half a mind to file a complaint with HR. We don't tolerate PTO abuse at this company, and that includes tacking on your *paid* lunch hour at the beginning or end of your time off. The lunch you just took should come out of your PTO."

Her argument was completely contrived and, under normal circumstances, wouldn't hold water. But this was Sue Ellen, and she always got her way. It was senseless trying to point out the fault in her logic—i.e. the fact that he had clocked in thirty minutes *before* lunch and therefore wasn't "tacking it onto his time off" like she claimed—because if she decided to submit a formal complaint to HR, no one would push back against her.

So, he did the only thing he could in the situation. Surrender.

"I'm sorry, Sue Ellen," he dropped his head submissively, "I promise I won't do anything like that again."

Sue Ellen grinned smugly at him giving him a nice view of the lipstick smeared on her front teeth. She was nasty with everybody, but Wyatt was almost positive that she derived a special kind of pleasure from making people taller than her cower. He'd watched her consistently pick on one of his old coworkers when he first joined the company. His name was Marcus. He was a good worker and easily the tallest person in the building. Eventually, he'd gotten so fed up with the bullying that he quit in the middle of his shift.

At the time, Wyatt had been proud of Marcus. But now that he was gone, Wyatt—who was six foot himself; a good eight inches taller than Sue Ellen—was a prime target. Knowing this, he worked extra hard to be an exemplary employee and avoid her wrath, and for the most part he succeeded, but she was the kind of person who could find fault with Santa Claus, an expert at building grudges out of nothing at all.

"You're damned right you won't," she said, pushing back a few graying red curls from her forehead with a plump hand. "Now get back to work."

Wyatt shuffled back to his miserable little cubicle wondering to himself if Sue Ellen still intended to file a complaint with HR or not. Fortunately, if they found him guilty of violating their PTO policies, a first-time offense wouldn't be enough to get him fired. Still, they might take that time out of his PTO just to satisfy Sue Ellen's bloodlust.

He sighed and ran a hand through his hair. His manager fucking sucked. This job fucking sucked. His coworkers were just as fucking sad and miserable as he was. And he was fucking tired of everything. His anger towards Andy from before felt miles away now. He understood the desperation that had driven him to FanFrenzy. And frankly, maybe Andy had made the right decision.

Wyatt would give anything to be happy again.

———

When Wyatt finally got home, he found that Andy had gotten them pizza and beers for dinner. This was a treat that they couldn't always afford to splurge on, but then again, Andy's disposable income wasn't what it used to be. Wyatt figured this was an apology pizza, and he was more than happy to accept it

"How was your day?" Andy asked, handing him a plate. "Aside from the train wreck this morning…" He seemed jittery, like he was nervous about something. Wyatt thought that they'd ended things on good terms earlier, but it seemed as though guilt was still eating at him.

"Eh, it was okay," Wyatt sighed and scooped up two large slices of pepperoni. Having skipped out on both breakfast and lunch, he was starving. "Sue Ellen gave me grief about taking lunch after coming into work late. Threatened to file a complaint with HR."

"*What?*" Andy's voice went up an octave. "Are you fucking serious?"

Wyatt shrugged. He still wasn't sure if she'd decide to take action or not. "I'd rather not talk about it."

Andy respected his wishes and avoided the topic of work for the rest of dinner. They sat in the living room watching sitcom reruns and chatting lightly. There was an obvious tension in the air as they both delicately tiptoed around the elephant in the room. Wyatt wondered if they would ever speak of the incident that morning ever again. Not that he was in any hurry to talk about it.

After they polished off most of the pizza and the six-pack of beer, Andy muted the television and turned to Wyatt on the couch.

"I, um, was wondering if I could talk with you about something?"

Wyatt didn't like the sound of that. This felt uncharacteristically formal for Andy. They never asked to have conversations with each other, they just *had* them.

"Uh, sure," he said.

"Okay, cool. Hang tight for a second." He scurried to his room, leaving Wyatt perplexed, and returned a moment later with his laptop. He plopped back down onto the couch and began, "So, um. This morning…"

Well, that answered Wyatt's question. Turned out they would be talking about the incident a lot sooner than he imagined.

"What about it?" he asked cautiously.

Andy shifted on his cushion, "Remember how I told you I had over seven hundred subscribers?"

He nodded. "Yes. Why?"

"Well, that number is now over five thousand."

Wyatt's mouth fell open. "Excuse me?"

"Yeah, see?" He spun his laptop around and showed Wyatt his subscriber total on his FanFrenzy profile. It read: *5,027 Fans!*

He began quickly doing the mental math, calculating the approximate annual salary based on this number of followers. It was in the ballpark of $482,000 *without tips*.

His mouth struggled to form words. "Wh— I don't— How... What *happened*?"

"My video from earlier apparently went viral."

"You mean of me walking in on you?"

Andy nodded his head. "Everyone's dying to find out what happens next."

Wyatt stared at him, dumbstruck. "Jesus, Andy, you must be making a fucking fortune right now."

"I know, it's crazy," he agreed. "I actually made a spreadsheet breaking down the hypothetical monthly and annual earnings based on the ten-dollar subscriptions and average tip rate. I took into account platform fees, too. Take a look."

He opened up a spreadsheet and turned his laptop toward him again. Wyatt looked it over and math was all sound. The projected twelve-month income was estimated at half a million dollars. *Half. A. Million.*

Wyatt stared at the spreadsheet for a long time, unable to think of what to say. He felt like his best friend just told him he won the lottery. On the one hand, he was insanely happy for Andy. But on the other, he couldn't help but think about his own shitty job. It would take him ten years to make the same amount of money that Andy would earn in just one. At this rate, Andy was bound to adopt a very different lifestyle from the one they'd been living. This conversation was probably about how he was looking for an apartment of his own now. Likely a fancy penthouse somewhere in the trendy district of the city

Wyatt gave him a weak smile. "Wow, that's great, man. Congratulations. You deserve it."

Andy gave an uncomfortable smile of his own and shifted in his seat again. "Thanks, dude. But, uh… See, the thing is, I'm not sure I'm going to be able to hold my audience's attention. And if I can't do that, then I'll start losing followers. So, this kind of success might not be a long-term thing."

Was he about to start asking him for advice on how to manage his porn career? Wyatt mentally groaned and shot a helpless glance toward the kitchen, wishing that they weren't out of beer.

"So, what are you gonna do?" he asked, trying to sound interested.

"Well, I've put a lot of thought into this, and I know that customer happiness is critical for success. And, um, as far as I can tell, there's really only one obvious answer to keeping the fans happy."

"And what's that?"

Andy's face had become a deep shade of red. He took a deep breath and finally said, "I think you should join me."

Wyatt's eyes bugged out of his skull. "*WHAT!?*"

"I-I know that sounds crazy but hear me out!"

"You're damn right that sounds crazy!" he said incredulously. "And here I thought nothing would ever be able to top the shock I had this morning! Good Lord, Andy—you think I should make *porn* with you!?"

"It's not like we'd be fucking each other! We'd just be two dudes getting naked on camera, jerking off and stuff. The gay-for-pay thing is a hot market! People eat it up!"

"Do you *hear* yourself right now? This is completely insane!"

Andy folded his arms. "Really? You think half a million dollars is insane?"

Wyatt opened his mouth to retort but then closed it again.

"I was planning to split everything fifty-fifty," Andy continued. "But hell, we could even do forty-sixty. I don't care! That would still be more than enough for me. And it would certainly be enough for you to quit your shitty job. This could be a good thing for both of us."

Wyatt squinted at him and frowned. "Don't pretend this is about me. You just want to make money."

He held out his arms and shrugged, "Yes, I *do* want to make money. Because I never want to work at Office Haven again or struggle to afford groceries. And once my twenty-fifth birthday rolls around, I'll no longer be able to use my parent's health insurance and I hear that shit is pretty fucking expensive. But don't you *dare* say that I don't care about you, Wyatt. Every single day I see how miserable you are and it fucking kills me. I just want us to both be happy like we used to be, and this might be the thing that gives us our freedom back."

Wyatt stared at him for a long time, letting his words sink in. The idea of escaping from his current job and saying goodbye to Sue Ellen forever was almost tempting enough to make him agree to this harebrained proposition right now.

But there were still so many issues with his plan. There was no way in hell it would work.

He sighed, "Andy, I appreciate you trying to think up solutions to my work problems. But this whole thing is just crazy. You have to admit that. I mean, it's *you and me* we're talking about. We're best friends for crying out loud. Do you really think that *we* could make porn together? Because I don't think I could even if I wanted to."

Andy rolled his eyes. "Dude, it's a *job*. That's it. Whatever we do on camera doesn't mean anything. Besides, wouldn't you prefer to do this with someone you know and are comfortable with rather than a stranger?"

"I'd prefer not to do this at all, but I suppose I get your point." A thought crossed his mind and squeezed his eyes shut, shaking his head, "I just don't think I could get on camera in the first place. What if someone recognized me? That could completely fuck up my chances of getting a job in the future.

"Dude, you might not need another job. This could be it!"

"There's no security in it, though! Sure, luck has been on your side lately, but it might not always be that way. Your success could dry up overnight. Then, what?"

Andy looked at him with a patient look. "Do you know how much the top model on FanFrenzy makes?"

"No…"

"Eleven million dollars. *A month*."

Wyatt stared at him in disbelief. "Are you serious?"

"Yes. And she's been pulling that in consistently for the past two years. Now, granted, women tend to do better on the site than guys do, statistically speaking, and the portion of models making seven figures a month is small. But we could be making six figures a month if we doubled my current follower count, which feels doable to me. And if we kept that up for four or five years, we could be retired before we're thirty!"

Wyatt smiled like a parent might smile at something naive their child said. "I like your enthusiasm, dude, but a lot goes into planning for retirement. Pretty sure FanFrenzy doesn't offer a 401k."

"No, but you're the finance guy. You're good with this sort of thing. If you saved up seven figures in a few years, you could invest the bulk of it and live off the interest. It's better to make large investments as early as possible and let your money work harder for you, right?"

…He was right. Wyatt furrowed his brows.

"Since when did you know so much about finance?"

"Did you think I'd walk into a pitch unprepared? I did my research! I knew what sorts of things you'd be worried about. You think I'd make spreadsheets just for the fun of it?"

Despite himself, Wyatt laughed. "Well, *I* would."

"I know you would," Andy grinned. "That's why I figured I should try to speak your language." He passed the laptop over to Wyatt and showed him the various tabs of the spreadsheet he'd created. There were different hypotheticals based on gradually increasing intervals of subscribers—5,000 vs 10,000 vs 15,000, etc. Andy had really done his homework.

"C'mon," Andy said softly after a moment. "Don't you think it's at least worth a try? Even if things flop, you'll still be able to find another job again. The chances of your future employers finding out about this are slim to none. But this could *be* something, Wyatt. And it's like the saying goes…fortune favors the bold."

Wyatt scrolled through the spreadsheets and bit his lip. Andy had made a very solid argument. Everything was spelled out in front of him in crisp, clean numbers. He couldn't believe he was admitting this to himself, but he was seriously considering this proposal.

No more forty-hour work weeks. No more being overworked and babysitting old dudes who should know better, he thought to himself. *And perhaps best of all, no more Sue Ellen.*

He swallowed and looked at Andy. His hazel eyes were eagerly searching his for an answer.

"I need to think about it," Wyatt said. Andy nodded seriously, but a big smile was spreading across his face. "What?"

"That's not a no," Andy said, full-on grinning now.

Wyatt rolled his eyes but couldn't help smiling back. "It still *could* be!"

"I know, I know. But you're actually giving this some thought. That's more than I was expecting, honestly. Thank you."

Wyatt shrugged awkwardly and looked away. "Thanks for going to all this trouble for me, I guess," he gestured to the laptop.

"And don't forget about the pizza," Andy added.

"Oh, so is *that* why we had pizza tonight? Buttering me up, huh?"

He grinned, "Duh."

Wyatt laughed and shoved his shoulder playfully. "Well, then you really should've gotten me dessert, too."

"I did," he said smugly. "There's a tube of chocolate chip cookie dough in the fridge. Shall I preheat the oven?"

Wyatt glared at him. "…Yes."

Chapter Five

The following day was a Friday, and Wyatt had left for work before Andy woke up. He still hadn't given him an answer yet, but Andy figured he'd need a couple of days at least. Hopefully, it wouldn't take more time than that, though. He was worried about his followers getting bored if he didn't give them an update soon. However, to some extent, the mystery seemed to be working in his favor because there was a steady trickle of new followers coming in throughout the day.

Andy rolled out of his bed, made a good breakfast, played video games for a bit, and then went to the gym to work out with Leslie. She asked him about the situation with his roommate, and he ended up spilling the beans about the conversation he'd had with Wyatt the night before.

"You asked your best friend and roommate to make *porn* with you?" she asked him incredulously. "Jesus Christ, what did he even say to that?"

"He said he had to think about it."

She raised her brows, looking impressed. "Huh. You must've made a strong case. Are you sure he's straight?"

"Yes!" he said, exasperatedly. "I've known him for years. He's strictly into women."

"Is he cute?"

Andy felt a hot flare of jealousy. Oddly, he couldn't exactly place where his jealousy was coming from. The idea of Leslie being interested in Wyatt really irked him—between the two of them, Andy felt that he was the more attractive one. But also, the idea of Wyatt being interested in Leslie bothered him even more. Maybe he was worried that Wyatt wouldn't have time for him anymore if he got a girlfriend. Yeah, that was probably it.

"Why do you care?" he asked, folding his arms.

She simply rolled her eyes. "I'm not interested in your roommate, dumbass. I have a boyfriend. His name is

Cameron. I was just curious if your roommate even had the right 'look' for porn."

"Oh," he said lamely. Had he known that Leslie had a boyfriend? He was pretty sure he didn't. Normally, he would've found this news disappointing, but honestly, he felt more relieved. "Well, I'm not the best judge for this sort of thing, but I'd say he's pretty handsome. He's tall, muscular, with sandy blond hair. He's got a good jaw, too. Oh! And he has nice eyes. They're a really nice blue color. Sometimes when the light hits them right, they look like blue gemstones or something."

"You mean sapphires?"

"Yeah! That's them!"

"Uh huh…" She was giving him a weird look.

"What?"

"Oh, nothing," she shrugged. "So, which one of you is gonna bottom?"

Andy's brain immediately supplied him with an answer: *Probably me since I took an eight-inch dildo up my ass like a champ and would gladly do it again.*

His mind then served him a mental image of Wyatt's face coupled with the memory of what it felt like having his ass stretched out by the dildo on his bed. His dick twitched in his gym shorts, and his face went a deep shade of red. The idea of him and Wyatt doing...*that* was completely and utterly wrong

"We wouldn't be doing that sort of thing!" he said indignantly.

Her face pinched in confusion. "Then what *are* you going be doing?"

Somehow trying to answer that question was more mortifying that imagining him and Wyatt fucking.

"J-Just other stuff!" he sputtered. "Like— You know... Stuff!"

She watched him with mild amusement and nodded slowly, "Oh, okay. 'Stuff.' Got it. Well, hopefully your fans like *stuff*."

His face was burning so intensely he thought he might actually be left with blisters on his cheeks. "Can we get back to the workout now?"

"Of course, Porn Star. I want twenty-five burpees. Go!"

———

That evening, Andy decided to assemble dinner again for both him and Wyatt. It wasn't a ploy to win him over, just a nice thing to do. On top of that, Andy had been anxiously awaiting his return from work, hoping that he had made up his mind about FanFrenzy, and needed an outlet for his nervous energy. So, he put together a simple salad using ingredients from the fridge—lettuce, tomatoes, shredded carrots, and vinaigrette. He also reheated the two remaining slices of pizza from the night before in the toaster oven. There would be no beer with tonight's entree, but they did still have cookies for dessert.

Andy, who had memorized Wyatt's schedule perfectly, just finished plating everything when he came through the door.

He called over his shoulder, "Hey, dude. How was your day?"

When he turned around, he was taken aback by how tired Wyatt looked. His shoulders sagged, his cheeks lacked their usual healthy color, his eyes were dull and defeated.

"Horrible," he mumbled. Then, he lifted his nose to the air and sniffed, his eyes regaining some of their spark. "Did you make dinner?"

"I just fancied up some leftovers, but yeah," he said, handing him a plate.

"Oh my God, you're amazing. I could kiss you. Thanks, dude."

They took their places at the bartop and tucked into their dinner. As they ate, Andy snuck sidelong glances at Wyatt. Food seemed to be improving his mood, but he still looked miserable.

"What happened today?" he asked.

Wyatt sighed and wiped his mouth with his napkin, "Sue Ellen happened."

"What did she do this time?"

"Well, she decided that she didn't want to let the lunch thing go from yesterday, so she informed me that she did file a complaint with HR and that they would be taking that hour from my PTO."

Andy gaped at him. "Are you fucking serious?"

"Yeah, but that's not the worst of it. It gets better. She then told me that she looked at our team's 'productivity report' for the week—whatever the fuck that means—and saw that I'm underperforming compared to everyone else. Which, of course, makes sense considering that I'm the only person who has taken time off this week. Obviously I haven't gotten as much work done as everyone else. But she said that this 'trend' was troubling to her, so she's putting me on a performance improvement plan."

Andy winced. He didn't like the sound of that. "What does that mean?"

"It means that for the next four pay periods, if any payroll discrepancies or complaints can be traced back to me, then I can be fired. I'm thorough with my work though, so I'm not worried about mistakes. However, I *do* have issues getting managers to give me their employee timesheets. When they fail to deliver on time, there's nothing I can do—it's out of my hands. But it means that their employees don't get their paycheck when they're supposed to. And of course, those complaints go directly to Sue Ellen."

"But they're not your fault. Do you really think she would fire you over them?"

"Oh, I know she would. That's just the kind of person she is. You want to hear something else fucked up? She waited until *after* I clocked out for lunch to call me into her office and have this meeting with me. It lasted for fifty fucking minutes. And just before it ended, she told me that if she caught me abusing my lunch hour again, it would result in my immediate termination. She said, 'If you're even a minute late, you're through!' Naturally, by the time I got out of her office, there wasn't time to go across the street and buy food. So, I didn't eat anything. Just went back to my desk and ended my lunch break early like a chump."

"Jesus Christ… That woman is fucking *horrible*. I'm sorry you have to deal with her."

"Thanks, man." Wyatt pushed his empty plate away and rested his forearms heavily on the counter. He looked exhausted.

Andy wanted to give him a good bro hug but decided against it. Instead, he asked, "Dessert?"

The corner of Wyatt's mouth quirked into a smile. "Yes please.

He took their dirty plates and put them in the sink, then retrieved the leftover cookies. Wyatt accepted them gratefully, and without needing to be asked, Andy poured them both glasses of milk.

They sat together at the bartop, silently enjoying their desserts. Andy wished to himself that he could do something more for Wyatt, but things were out of his hands. He had already offered him an out from his shitty job, but it was up to Wyatt to decide whether or not he wanted to accept the offer. Andy wouldn't push him on it.

Typically on a Friday night, they would dive into video games or a movie after dinner, but Wyatt stayed seated and quiet after finishing the last cookie. Andy sat with him, wondering if he should say something or let the silence carry on.

Finally, just as Andy was starting to get fidgety, Wyatt turned to him and said, "I'll do it."

He blinked, confused. "What?

"The FanFrenzy thing. I'll do it." Wyatt was staring down intently at his hands.

A big, disbelieving smile stretched across Andy's face from ear to ear. "Holy shit, dude. Are you sure?"

Wyatt lifted his head to meet Andy's eyes and nodded.

"Dude, holy *shit*!" Andy let out a string of giddy laughter. "This is amazing! Thank you! So, are we settled on forty-sixty? Or do you want more?"

Wyatt waved a hand at him, "Don't be ridiculous. We're doing this thing fifty-fifty."

His grin stretched even wider. "You're my fucking hero, dude. Do you know that? Thank you for doing this."

"Yes, I've agreed to do it, *but*," Wyatt said firmly, "only as a trial. I'll give it one month to see how things go. And

I'm not quitting my job before I know with some certainty that this could work out."

"Understood."

"And also, we need to talk about what this entails for me. I'm not sucking any dicks."

"Fair enough," Andy said. "We don't have to take things too far, but you do know that we'll have to be naked together, right?"

Color rose in Wyatt's cheeks, but he nodded.

"And we'll have to be hard in front of each other, too."

He nodded again, "Yeah, I figured that much."

"Also, I know the fans will want to see us interact with each other a little bit. Would you be comfortable with me jerking you off at some point?"

Wyatt's ears were burning red now. "I guess so."

"Okay," Andy spoke lightly as if worried about scaring him away. "And what about you jerking me off?"

He buried his face in his hands and mumbled, "Maybe…"

Andy wasn't exactly reassured by this. Ideally, they would gradually push their comfort zones with each other every month to keep their fans interested. While there were certainly lines in the sand that they wouldn't cross, they had to be willing to be somewhat adventurous if this was going to work.

"Are you sure about this? Because if you're not comfortable, that's okay, man. You don't have to do anything you don't want to."

Wyatt whirled around, a pained look etched onto his face, "But I *do* want to. I want this to work, Andrew. I want to get the hell out of my job and never have to worry about Sue Ellen or any other petty corporate bullshit ever again."

"Alright," he said, squaring his shoulders with determination, "then we need to be willing to stretch beyond our comfort zones a little and actually *do* this damn thing, okay? Half-assing it isn't an option."

Wyatt swallowed. "You're right."

"Then let's practice."

His eyes widened, filled with terror. "Right now?"

"Chill out. I'm not asking you to go from zero to sixty. We just need to make sure we've got the basics down first."

"And what are the basics?" he asked nervously.

"Being naked around each other."

Wyatt seemed to think on this and then relaxed slightly. "That's not too bad."

"Right," Andy agreed. "It's nothing we haven't already seen before."

They'd seen each other naked several times, the first time being within the first two weeks of knowing each other. As part of their hazing ritual, all of the pledges had to sneak onto the football field at night and streak across it. The next time was during their sophomore on a camping trip they'd taken over Spring Break. All of the frat brothers went skinny dipping in the nearby lake, just because.

It hadn't been awkward then, so it shouldn't be too awkward now. Sure, the context was very different this time, but they weren't crossing any new boundaries yet.

"So, let's do it," Andy said plainly, sliding off his chair and walking into the living room where they had more space. Wyatt followed him sheepishly.

They stood facing each other, several feet apart. Andy knew he was going to have to take the lead, so he pulled off his shirt in one smooth motion. Then, without any fanfare, he slid his fingers under the waistband of his basketball shorts and boxers and push them down, letting them crumple to the ground around his ankles. A few months ago, he couldn't imagine doing something like this in front of his best friend, but his time spent making porn had apparently made him more comfortable with nudity.

He stuck his arms out at his sides as if to say *tada*. Wyatt's eyes immediately drifted upward to the ceiling, and his blush had returned with a vengeance.

Andy sighed. "Dude, come *on*. It's my dick, not fucking Medusa. You can look at it!"

"I don't want to look at it!"

"But you've seen it before!"

"Like a brief glimpse. This is different. I don't want to stare at it directly!"

"Well, you have to! This is Step One. If you can't even do this, there's no way you're cut out to be on FanFrenzy."

Wyatt groaned but finally dropped his head with his eyes squeezed shut. Then, he opened one of them like someone peaking at the screen during a horror movie.

"See?" Andy asked patiently. "Nothing bad happened."

Wyatt opened both eyes and blinked a few times. Just as Andy had predicted, he seemed thoroughly unbothered. Just stared at Andy with mild interest.

"Huh," he said. "It's just a penis."

Andy burst out laughing. "Yep, Wyatt. It's just a penis."

"This isn't so bad."

"I told you!" he said, putting his hands on his hips. "Now it's your turn."

"Oh, right..." Wyatt looked around nervously, shifting his weight from one foot to the other. Then, he slowly kicked off his shoes and pulled off his socks before working very carefully on the buttons of his shirt.

Andy knew that he was stalling; he wanted to shake him by the shoulders and tell him to rip off the fucking bandaid already. Dragging it out wouldn't help! But he kept his mouth shut and waited. If Wyatt wanted to take things slow, he would let him.

Finally, Wyatt reached the bottom button and shed the shirt. Then he unfastened his belt and shimmied out of his khakis. Next, he pulled off his undershirt. All that was left were his briefs. He glanced around the room one last time as if looking for something to save him, but when he found nothing, he sighed and pushed his underwear down to the carpet.

Andy checked him over from head to toe. He'd seen Wyatt in the buff before, but he hadn't looked at him critically until now. He was thinking about the conversation he'd had earlier with Leslie. *I was just curious if your roommate even had the right 'look' for porn.*

After giving him the once over, Andy decided that he did have the right look. He was tall and handsome and in decent shape for how infrequently he worked out. He had nice pecs, well-defined arms, and strong thighs. Just good proportions overall. Also, he had a sexy little trail of blond fur leading down from his belly button to his pubes. The fans would appreciate that, Andy thought. He also couldn't help but notice that Wyatt had a big, heavy set of balls. The fans were *definitely* going to appreciate that.

Wyatt also stuck his arms out at his sides. *Tada.*

Andy smiled. "Step One complete!" Then, he took a step forward and extended his hand. "Nice to meet you, Naked Wyatt."

Wyatt looked at him like he had two heads and then laughed. "You can't be serious right now."

"Dead serious!"

He rolled his eyes but couldn't hide his smile. Then, he shook Andy's hand, "Nice to meet you too, Naked Andy."

Andy's grin broadened even more, "Step Two complete!"

"Huh?" Wyatt gave him a puzzled look.

"Step One was getting used to being naked around each other," he said. "Step Two was getting used to touching each other while naked. And you handled it like a pro! Well done.

Wyatt looked pleased with himself and seemed to be gaining confidence. "What's Step Three?"

"Getting hard around each other."

The confidence (and color) left Wyatt's face. "I don't know about that, dude…"

"Well, we're gonna be hard on camera so…"

"I know, I know. But it's just us right now. Isn't that weird?"

"It's only weird if you make it weird! Look, it's not going to be any easier to get it up when you know that thousands of strangers are watching you. The whole point of this is to practice in a pressure-free environment. If we aren't able to complete Step Three tonight, then it's no big deal. We can try again later."

After chewing on Andy's words for a moment, Wyatt sighed and dragged his hands down his face. "You're right. This is what practice is for."

"Atta boy," Andy smiled. Then he walked over to the couch, took a seat, and patted the cushion next to him. "Try not to be so tense. It's just two bros jerking off."

Wyatt froze on his way to the couch. "Wait. Step Four isn't busting a nut around each other, is it?"

He laughed. "I don't think we should worry about Step Four today. Three is enough."

"I'm okay with that," Wyatt said dropping down onto the couch. "How are you so chill about this though?"

"I don't know," he shrugged. "I guess doing porn helped me to realize that sex doesn't have to mean anything."

"That's kind of sad, don't you think?" Wyatt was a romantic at heart. He'd never had sex with anyone who he didn't have strong feelings for.

"It's not like I *can't* have meaningful sex ever again. I've just learned to compartmentalize the FanFrenzy stuff." Andy started tugging casually on his cock.

"Are you sure though? I mean you haven't had a date since Fall Semester of senior year. What if this porn thing has changed things and you just don't know it?" Wyatt had unconsciously started copying Andy's movements and tugging on his own dick.

"I doubt it," he said. "I mean, when I jerk off, I still fantasize about the same stuff." That wasn't entirely true. He was now much more interested in ass play than he ever imagined he would be. Every time he masturbated now, he imagined someone fucking him with a dildo or strap-on. Wyatt didn't need to know that, though.

"But what if your date has a problem with you doing porn?"

"Then it wasn't meant to be," Andy shrugged. "I want to be with someone who loves me as I am. No judgment."

Wyatt hummed thoughtfully. "I want that, too. Dating can be such a headache. Always worrying about saying something stupid or whether my hobbies are interesting enough. I just want to be with someone who *gets* me, you know? Someone who's easy to be with."

"Exactly! Someone who likes the same movies and shows that I do and doesn't make me watch weird shit. There are only so many art house movies I can force myself to sit through."

Wyatt laughed, "Right! And someone who likes hanging around and playing video games on the weekend instead of spending all day going to different antique stores."

"*Yes!* And then maybe things get a little sexual after a while. I've always wanted to get a blowjob while playing video games."

"Dude, me too! That's been a fantasy of mine for so long. I don't even know why, but it just sounds hot."

"What other fantasies do you have?

"I don't really have any besides that... I guess I'm just vanilla."

"Oh, come on, Wyatt. I know there must be other stuff you've always wanted to try."

"Well..."

"Yes?

"I don't want to say... It's kind of embarrassing."

"Let me guess. Is it anal?"

"..."

"Fucking knew it."

"But how did you know!?"

"Because *every* guy wants to try anal! It's way tighter and supposed to feel amazing.

"So, does that mean that you also want to try it?"

Andy had, of course, always wanted to try it—just like every other straight guy his age—but his definition of "anal" was broader now than it was before. He still wanted to try anal as a top, but if he had the choice and was being completely honest with himself, he would choose to try bottoming first. Ever since he'd discovered the wonders of his prostate, he couldn't get enough of it. But again, Wyatt didn't need to know that.

"Of course, dude," he said. It was then that he realized that he'd managed to get himself fully hard. He glanced over at Wyatt's package and *JESUS CHRIST!* Apparently, Wyatt was a grower because he was fucking *huge.* Just looking at him, he was probably a good inch longer than his dildo. Maybe more. Also, he was definitely thicker than the dildo was. Andy's hole throbbed at the sight of it.

"Holy shit, dude," he mumbled. "You're hung like a horse."

Wyatt's eyes went wide as he looked down at his own fully hard erection. Then, he glanced over at Andy's boner and quickly directed his eyes toward the ceiling again, removing his hand from his cock and letting fall heavily across his thigh with a small *plap*.

"Oh my God, I can't believe this is happening." His ears went a bright red color.

"Calm down, dude. Relax. This was exactly the point of the exercise. We completed Step Three!

Wyatt looked at him, chewing on his bottom lip anxiously. "We did?"

"Dude, yeah! And you were great. Don't freak yourself out now. We're done."

"So, what happens now?"

"Well, I was thinking we could play a few rounds of *Speed Trap Turbo.*"

"No, I mean, what other steps are there before we go live on FanFrenzy? How much practice do you think I need?"

Andy shrugged. "I think you're probably good to go at this point."

"What!? But the real thing is going to be much more…*involved* than this was, right? I don't think I'm prepared for that!"

He turned on the couch to face Wyatt, "I get that you're nervous, dude, but that's part of the appeal for the fans. They want to watch you step outside of your comfort zone and try new things for the first time. We don't want to over-prepare for this. Otherwise, it won't come off as genuine. The whole reason my profile has gotten so popular is because you walked in on me during a live stream and it *wasn't* scripted. People can tell when something is authentic or not.

Wyatt continued to gnaw on his lip nervously.

"Think of it this way," Andy continued. "You don't have to worry about doing a 'good' job because people just want to see the real story unfold. If the first couple of times are awkward, it's not a big deal, okay? People will expect that. So, don't stress too much about it."

Finally, Wyatt released his bottom lip from his teeth and let out a breath. "That makes me feel a bit better... Thanks."

"No prob," he smiled. "Now how about a race on *Speed Trap*?"

"Yeah, that sounds good. But, uh, can I put my clothes back on?"

Andy got up to turn on the TV and the SwitchBox console, "Only if you want to."

Wyatt seemed to think on this for a moment, his eyes shifting back and forth between his pile of clothes on the floor and the TV screen. Both of their erections were long gone at this point.

"Actually, this is fine," he said finally.

Andy was a bit surprised by that but played it cool. If Wyatt wanted to continue practicing Step One, then good for him. He bypassed his own clothes on his way back to the couch and handed Wyatt a controller, "Player Two picks the course."

And so, like two best bros who were totally comfortable in their bodies and secure in their relationship, they played naked video games together. It was surprisingly easy.

Chapter Six

"Hey guys! Sorry it's been a while since I've posted anything new. It's been a crazy couple of days as I'm sure most of you could guess."

Wyatt stood in the threshold of Andy's bedroom, watching from the sidelines as he started a new FanFrenzy live stream. He addressed everyone with an easiness that Wyatt found admirable. Today's stream was a big deal not only because it was the first one Andy had done since getting caught in Wyatt's room, but also because Wyatt would be introducing himself to the audience for the first time ever. He was fidgeting nervously, unsure what to do with his body, as he waited for Andy's cue to join him in front of the camera.

It was Sunday, only two days after their little practice run on the couch. Since then, they had not explored anything beyond Steps One and Two. Andy had decided to spend all of Saturday naked. He simply walked out of his room in the morning without a stitch on and proceed about his day like usual. Wyatt got the picture and quickly followed suit, shedding his pajamas in favor of something infinitely more breathable. His initial feelings of shyness quickly melted away thanks to how casual Andy had been about everything. He made it feel like the most normal and natural thing in the world.

As the day went on, Wyatt realized that there was something very nice about walking around the apartment totally free and open. It was a level of comfort with his environment that he'd never felt before. What's more, he realized that he'd never been closer with anyone in his life than he was with Andy. Trying to imagine this kind of relationship with any of his other friends was impossible.

Now though, he felt shy again. But this time it wasn't about Andy so much as the *thousands* of strangers that would be watching them. He tried to remind himself of the reason he was doing this—freedom. This was his ticket out of his shithole job and away from Sue Ellen. Whatever discomfort he felt at that moment was a small price to pay.

"...and we ended up having a *looong* talk about everything," Andy was saying. "When he found out I had a FanFrenzy account he was shocked, of course. I mean, who wouldn't be in his situation, right? But eventually, he got used to the idea and then he started asking me questions about it. When I told him how curious you guys were about him, he became even more interested. Anyway, long story short, it took a lot of convincing, but he said that he was willing to join me on a stream to see what it was like to do a show for you guys. Keep in mind, he's never done anything like this before, so please go easy. But what do you say? Do you wanna meet him? He's here right now."

Andy leaned forward slightly to read the chat. Wyatt couldn't see it from where he was standing, but Andy's face lit up in a bright grin.

"I'll take that as a yes," he said. "Alright, then. Please welcome my roommate—Jack!"

Heart racing wildly, Wyatt shuffled from his spot by the door over to Andy's bed to take a seat next to him. He looked at the laptop sitting on the desk in front of them and saw only a preview window of Andy and himself sitting side by side. Huh. This wasn't as bad as he thought it would be. He half expected to see people looking back at them, jerking off in their creepy, dimly lit rooms. But there was none of that. It was only the video of them and a chat window on the righthand side. Wyatt could barely make out what the chat was saying, it was moving so quickly.

"Don't be shy, Jack," Andy said. "You can say hi."

It took him a split second to remember that he was Jack. That was the only good name they could think of that fit with Ace's deck-of-cards theme.

Wyatt sat up straighter and waved awkwardly at the computer, "Hello."

"How are you feeling?" asked Andy.

"A bit nervous, to be honest," he laughed.

"Don't be. You've already made a good impression with everyone." Andy nodded toward the chat, grinning.

Wyatt leaned forward a bit to see what everyone was saying.

THAT'S YOUR ROOMMATE!?

Holy fuck he's fine as hell!

Omg what a hottie! <3

God is REAL!!

Hey daddyyyyy ;)

VERY nice to meet you Jack. Just, wow!

I wish my roommate was a fraction as cute as you are lol

Love the sexy accent stud

PLEASE tell me we get to see him naked...

Wyatt felt his cheeks growing warm, "Y'all are gonna make me blush. You're too sweet."

"Yeah, jeez, they're really laying the flattery on thick. I'm starting to feel jealous," Andy teased.

In response, messages started pouring in showering Andy with praise:

We haven't forgotten about you Ace!!

No one could ever replace you <3

Ace 4ever!!!

You're still my number 1 ;-)

"Aww, thanks guys," he smiled. "I appreciate the love. I've really missed everyone over the last couple of days. But today is about our guest of honor, not me. So, I thought we'd start out with a little Q&A! Go ahead and send in your burning questions for Jack."

Andy watched the chat closely and picked out select questions from the incoming flood for Wyatt to answer. He read one aloud, "What was it like catching your roommate in your bed?"

Wyatt chuckled, "Well, it definitely came as a shock. And after the initial surprise, I was pretty pissed, I'll be honest. But when I found out the reason behind it, I chilled out."

Andy read out another: "Had you ever seen Ace naked before that?"

"Um, once or twice, yeah. We meet back in school and have lived together for a few years now. So, I've seen him naked on occasion. But nothing like *that* though."

Andy pinked slightly and laughed. "Yeah, I think that experience scarred both of us honestly. Next question says, Have you ever been with a guy before?"

"Nope," he shook his head. "I'm straight."

"Someone else asks, Would you ever experiment with a guy?"

"Well, this whole thing is an experiment for me, so I guess the answer to that is yes."

"How far would you be willing to go with a dude?"

Wyatt looked thoughtful as he considered the question. "I'd probably let a guy go down on me, but I don't think I'd enjoy it very much."

"Would *you* ever go down on a guy?"

"Never say never. But probably not."

"Have you ever tasted your own cum before?"

He blushed, but said, "Hasn't every guy?"

"Would you rather be too hot or too cold?"

"Oh! An innocent question—that's nice. Too cold."

"Tits or ass?"

"And we're back at it... Ass."

"Where's the weirdest place you've ever had sex?"

"Hmm. Does jerking off count as sex?"

Andy shrugged, "Sure, why not?"

"In that case, I'd have to say it was one time in the car while driving."

"Really?" Andy's eyebrows went up. "You jerked off while *driving*?"

"Yeah," he laughed shyly, scratching the back of his neck. "I was driving back home one summer, and I got bored on one of the country roads. There was nothing around for miles, so I just rubbed one out."

"Didn't that make a huge mess?"

"Oh, absolutely. I immediately regretted it and had to pull over to clean everything up. There are still some stains on my seatbelt strap from it, but you probably wouldn't notice them." He smirked at Andy, "Anyway, I thought *they* were supposed to be asking the questions right now, not you."

"Oh right! Sorry," he looked back at the screen. "Here's one: How big is your dick?"

"Eh, I'm average."

Andy let out a sharp, derisive laugh. "You are *not* average! I saw it once, you guys. It's fucking huge."

Wyatt's ears went red, "I might be a tiny bit bigger than average, but it's not huge! Stop exaggerating."

"Believe me, I'm *not*. You're hung, dude."

He'd never considered himself to be big before, but then again he hadn't spent much time comparing his penis with other guys. On Friday, he saw Andy's boner up close for the first time, and while yes, he was a bit bigger than him, he didn't think he was *that* much bigger. But now he was starting to second-guess himself. Maybe he *was* well-endowed... How could he have gone his entire life not realizing something like that?

It was then that he remembered his exes from college. All three of them had said at some point in their relationship that taking all of him was uncomfortable. At the time, Wyatt figured that it was a common issue that all couples faced. It never occurred to him that *he* was the problem—not until now anyway.

He suddenly felt embarrassed for being so oblivious and folded his arms. "Whatever, man," he said.

"Now everyone is asking if they can see it," Andy chuckled.

"I'm not just gonna whip it out."

Andy spoke into the camera, "Right. Since this is Jack's first time, we've decided to take things slow. So, I've set up a few tip goals that we can work toward. At a hundred dollars we'll strip to our underwear, at two hundred we'll get completely naked, and at three hundred we'll jerk off. That way Jack has time to warm up a little first before getting naked. How does that sound?" He leaned forward to the laptop and clicked the button to launch the tip goal counter.

Almost immediately, dozens of donations flooded in, and they exceeded their top goal by several hundred dollars. Andy blinked, eyes wide, and turned to Wyatt who stared at the screen with a similar look of shock and surprise. Then, he threw back his head and started cackling. The absurdity of the situation was almost enough to make Wyatt laugh too, but the knowledge of what was coming next made him far too nervous.

"Well, so much for taking things slow. Sorry, Jack, but the people have decided your fate."

"You guys suck," he mumbled, hoping he didn't sound as anxious as he felt.

Andy got up and pulled his t-shirt off. Wyatt stood and followed his lead, albeit at a much slower pace. In a matter

124

of seconds, Andy had finished stripping off every bit of clothing he had on and was smiling at the camera, idly running a hand over his abs. Wyatt felt self-conscious. He was decently fit himself, but he didn't have sculpted abs like that. When it was just him and Andy hanging around the apartment naked together, he hadn't thought twice about the differences in their physiques. But now that they had an audience, he couldn't help but make comparisons. Andy was lean and well-defined, had good hair, and a really nice butt. Even Wyatt could appreciate how round and perky it was. On top of his all-around good-looking body, Andy also had an attractive personality. He was outgoing and charismatic and had a dazzling smile that could melt even the coldest heart. And when he laughed, the corners of his eyes would crease in a way that Wyatt had always found charming.

He swallowed. Standing next to Andy, he felt completely inadequate.

"Thank you, guys, for helping us reach our goals so quickly. Honestly, I can't believe how fast that happened. We're really feeling the love right now. Right, Jack?"

Wyatt tried smiling as convincingly as he could, "Absolutely." Then, he shimmied out of his jeans and took one deep, steadying breath before finally shucking his briefs.

The group chat erupted with compliments.

WOOF!

Ur fucking gorgeous Jack <3

Holy hell, you're perfect!

Yummy yummy ;)

Nice balls bro

You two look amazing together~

You boys have got me horny af right now

"If you think he looks good now, just wait until he's hard. I'm telling you, it's like a third leg."

Wyatt rolled his eyes and smiled despite himself—the praise he'd gotten from the chat seemed to soothe his ego. "God, would you shut up?" He gave him a playful shove.

126

Andy grinned and pushed him back, "Well, it's true!"

They continued to shove and tease each other until finally locking arms and pretending to wrestle. Andy's eyes twinkled with a boyish playfulness that had an infectious quality on Wyatt. They giggled and tussled, taunting each other and working to get the upper hand without actually exerting too much effort. Finally, Wyatt, who was bigger and stronger, managed to pull Andy into a headlock, but he retaliated by tickling his ribs.

Wyatt barked out a surprised laugh and immediately let him go. "You little shit! So, that's how you want to play is it?"

Andy backed away from him with arms outstretched, his face a giddy shade of pink. He was panting and laughing and shaking his head, "No, no, no!"

Wyatt lunged forward anyway and attacked the sensitive skin of Andy's sides. Andy cried out, giggling hysterically and trying to wriggle away, but Wyatt's strong arms had him trapped. He was so preoccupied with their little game of conquest that he didn't even realize that he had Andy's naked body pinned against his own.

Eventually, Andy was able to weasel out of his grasp and back away. "Truce! Truce!" he shouted, then extended one hand as a peace offering and inched closer cautiously.

Wyatt was flushed and panting, too. He'd been having so much fun he'd almost forgotten that they were naked and recording a live stream on a porn site. Then he remembered that they had fans watching and waiting. They had a mission to complete, so he accepted Andy's hand and shook it. "Truce."

They turned to the chat, and Andy said, "Sorry, guys. We got distracted."

LOL get his ass, Jack!

Wtf why are you guys so cute together!?

Y'all are adorable lol

Anyone else getting a gay vibe from this..?

I could watch you boys wrestle all day ;)

That was lowkey really hot lmao

Sooo are you guys gonna jerk off or what? xD

"Yes, we're still going to jerk off," Andy chuckled. "Hold your horses." He started pulling casually on his cock while continuing to read the incoming messages. Wyatt copied him, hoping to God that he would actually be able to get hard under pressure.

Andy laughed at a few of the comments and gave snappy replies every now and then, keeping the audience engaged. Somehow, while busy reading the chat and being an entertaining host, he managed to get a full hard-on. Upon seeing this, Wyatt's forehead broke out into a cold sweat. He barely had a semi and it had taken considerable effort to get it this far. Despite his best efforts, he couldn't distract himself from the fact that thousands of people were watching.

"Oh, they've got another question for you, Jack. They want to know if you've ever jerked off around other guys before."

"No, I can't say I have. This'll be a first." He didn't think that their practice session on Friday counted.

Andy got quiet for a moment as he caught up with the most recent messages. When he spoke again, there was surprise in his voice, "Oh! Someone just asked if I would jerk you off for the right price." He looked at Wyatt with a questioning look in his eyes and shrugged, "I mean, depending on the price, I wouldn't say no…"

Wyatt wasn't exactly sure if he was comfortable with that, but he didn't want to be the party pooper. If Andy was cool with it, then he was, too.

"Uh, sure. What price?"

Andy looked back at the screen, "Well, currently our tip total is just under six hundred bucks. So, how about this—if we manage to reach a thousand in the next hour, I'll jerk him off. Otherwise, we're busting a nut solo 'cause we can't wait all day."

Immediately, the computer chimed. A new donation had come through.

"Holy shit…" Andy stared at the screen. "Well, Jack, it looks like we hit our target again, thanks to a very generous donation from… Oh, look who it is! Str8boyaddict strikes again!" He turned to Wyatt, "He's the one who paid me to jerk off in your bed."

"Oh, gee. Thanks for that, pal," he snarked and watched as a new message from str8boyaddict appeared in the chat.

You're very welcome, Jack. Seeing as it ultimately led to this moment, I'd say it was worth every penny.

"Well, thank you, str8boy. We appreciate your donation," Andy said. Then he turned around to face Wyatt and—despite the glimmer of uncertainty in his eyes—said with a grin, "Are you ready for the best handjob of your life?"

Wyatt rolled his eyes. "Don't make promises you can't keep, son."

The chat window filled with laughing emojis, and he felt his ego swell. Normally, he wasn't one to give social media much thought, but he suddenly understood how the validation and attention could become addictive.

"Alright, smart ass, prepare to eat your words," Andy shot back, grabbing a nearby bottle of lube. He took a step closer, poured a bit into his palm, and then looked him in the eye. There was the briefest of pauses between them, and Wyatt knew that he was also second-guessing this decision.

But the moment quickly passed, and Andy reached forward and wrapped a hand around his semi-hard cock. Wyatt had unconsciously tensed his shoulders, but after the split-second panic of *Oh God my best friend is touching my dick*, he relaxed. It wasn't as unpleasant as he thought it would be. Someone else's hand was on his junk—that's all. No biggie.

Andy worked the lube all along his shaft and started tugging slowly, deliberately, as if trying to milk something out of him. It actually felt pretty good. Wyatt hadn't had any form of intimate contact with another human being since he'd been dumped during the last semester of senior year. This wasn't how he imagined his next handjob would play out, but his dick wasn't complaining. It was rapidly swelling in Andy's firm and competent grip. *Fuck...*

His eyes fell closed as Andy worked his hand over his head. An involuntary sigh rumbled in the back of his throat. So far, this wasn't the "best handjob of his life," but it surprisingly wasn't the worst.

In response to Wyatt's moan, Andy picked up his pace slightly. Wyatt opened his eyes and looked into Andy's— they stared back with an intensity he'd never seen before. His pupils were large, compressing the pretty hazel color of his irises into thin rings. A deep blush had spread from one cheek, over the bridge of his nose, to the other. His lips were parted slightly as if about to say something.

Wyatt's eyes landed on those lips and refused to look away. There was something oddly captivating about them. It was as if he was seeing them for the first time. They were plump and pink and looked soft.

His concentration was broken when Andy cleared his throat and mumbled something.

"Huh?" Wyatt asked.

"I said I'm going to try a different angle." Then he dropped to his knees so that Wyatt's dick was practically in his face and started pumping him with his fist

Oh, fuck! Wyatt's head rolled back, and a very audible moan escaped his mouth. Embarrassment hit him like a ton of bricks; his head snapped up in an instant, and he looked down at Andy with wide eyes.

Andy merely smiled a smug smile, and said, "I must be doing a pretty good job."

Jesus this was mortifying. Wyatt glanced at the laptop and could see his face turning bright red in the video preview window, which only made it worse. The humiliation should've been a total boner-killer, but Andy continued stroking his cock with a surprising amount of skill and it frankly felt incredible. He was hard as a rock. Why was Andy so good at this? Maybe guys were just inherently better at handling dick…? He wasn't sure, but the 'why' didn't really matter.

He stared down at Andy who was looking up at him. For a brief moment, he was taken aback by the surreality of seeing his best friend like this—on his knees, looking up at him, stroking his cock mere inches from his face. Wyatt could see Andy's own hard-on standing at attention between his legs. His thoughts went fuzzy.

"How do you guys think I'm doing for my first time?" Andy asked the chat. Wyatt hadn't been paying attention to the messages at all. It was hard to focus on much of anything right now. Andy responded to the messages, "Aww, thanks, guys. I appreciate it. And yeah, I'd say he's enjoying it, too." He looked up at him with a shit-eating grin.

"Oh, shut up," Wyatt mumbled.

Then, the computer chimed again. Another donation had come through. It was for another two hundred and fifty dollars. Below that was a message from the donor—str8boyaddict.

Put your mouth on it.

Wyatt barely had time to mentally process the meaning of the message, before looking down in horror to see Andy lunging toward his cock, mouth gaping like a sea bass. Everything was moving in slow motion, and he could do nothing but watch as the tip of his dick disappeared into Andy's mouth where it was immediately met with a delicious wet warmth that sent a shock of surprise and pleasure up his spine. Andy gracelessly continued down the length of his shaft until Wyatt felt himself hit the back of his throat.

Time suddenly began moving normally again as Andy's eyes widened with panic and he began choking and sputtering on the dick he'd dived mouth-first onto. Wyatt jumped backward, unsheathing himself, and Andy erupted into a vicious coughing fit.

"Dude, what the fuck!?" Wyatt snapped.

Red-faced and eyes watering, Andy continued coughing and waved his hands vaguely as words were clearly out of the question at the moment. Wyatt put his hands on his hips and impatiently waited for him to regain some composure. They had *not* talked about the possibility of blowjobs ahead of time.

Finally, Andy croaked, "Sorry, sorry. That was embarrassing…"

"I can't believe you just put your mouth on my dick, dude!"

"Sorry, I didn't think it would be a big deal. I mean *I* was the one doing it."

"We still should've talked about it first."

"You're right, you're right. I'm sorry, dude… It won't happen again." Beneath his wet and croaky voice, Andy was being sincere, and Wyatt knew it.

He wanted to stay mad at him, but he couldn't. Yes, they should've talked about it first, but he knew that Andy just got caught up in the moment. The only thing he was truly mad at was himself for enjoying the brief sensation of his best friend's mouth on him. That was *not* okay. He had evidently gone far too long without getting laid

"It's fine," he mumbled. "Just ask me next time…"

"I promise I will." Then he turned to the screen, "New rule guys: Please don't send us money for requests until we've agreed on the request first. Okay, str8boy? Also, sorry that was a total fail…"

Str8boy responded:

Understood. Also, no need to apologize. You did well for your first time, Ace. Just a little overeager.

"That's putting it mildly," Wyatt quipped.

Andy shrugged and laughed, "What can I say? I'm the kind of person who throws himself into things headfirst."

"You can say *that* again," he chuckled.

Andy shuffled a little closer to Wyatt and nodded to his still-hard dick. "Shall we get back to it?"

"Yeah, okay…" Wyatt met him in the middle again so that they were positioned appropriately in front of the camera.

"I'm gonna give you a bit more lube because I think most of it is in my mouth now," Andy said, wiping his mouth and grimacing.

Once his palm was slicked up, he grabbed Wyatt's cock again and began stroking him with the same competent grip as before. Wyatt's eyes fluttered shut. He begged his thoughts to take him elsewhere, trying to imagine that it was a hot brunette touching him instead, but his mind supplied him with the memory of Andy on his knees, looking up at him, pink lips hovering dangerously near to his cock head. It was a mental image that should've sunk his arousal like the

137

Titanic, but it didn't. It simply coalesced with the pleasure surging through his body. These two disparate things became enmeshed together, creating a confusion within him unlike anything he'd ever experienced. His best friend shouldn't be making him feel this good, and yet...

His hips began to move involuntarily, thrusting ever-so-slightly into his fist. Andy, who was focusing on the group chat and responding to messages, didn't seem to notice.

He laughed somewhere far away. "You guys are the worst! How did you already create a gif of my failed blowjob attempt!?"

Lost in the sensation of his hand, Wyatt barely heard him. Then, Andy said something else.

"Oh, double fist? That's a good idea."

Suddenly, Wyatt felt Andy's other hand close around his shaft, and he opened his eyes in surprise. He stared down at Andy as his fists began working him in a double-twisting motion, and *holy hell*. A small groan escaped his throat, and he bucked more noticeably.

Andy grinned up at him, "How is it?"

Brows pinched together in delirious pleasure, Wyatt simply nodded an affirmative.

"It must be good guys," he laughed and turned back to the chat.

Self-control was running thin, and Wyatt could no longer stop himself from rocking his hips needily into Andy's hands. From the base of his groin, he could feel pressure building within him which could only mean one thing—his orgasm was imminent. It was approaching at an alarming rate, and some distant part of Wyatt's mind reasoned that his lack of sex recently had weakened his stamina. All of a sudden, he knew he was past the point of no return.

"Ace..." he breathed. But Andy didn't hear him. He was too distracted with the chat, chuckling at something someone had posted. He tried again, this time with a greater sense of urgency. "*Ace.*"

Andy turned and started to say, "What is it, Jack?" but was abruptly cut off as Wyatt's hips stuttered and jerked before shooting a hot load all over his face. His orgasm tore through him with an intensity he hadn't expected, and he could do nothing but ride the ripples of electricity and watch as he pumped rope after rope of release onto his best friend.

Wyatt had, fortunately, missed his eyes, but he could not say the same for Andy's open mouth. Andy's eyes had gone wide with shock at first but then he clamped them shut, along with his mouth, as he helplessly held onto Wyatt's cock and let him finish.

When it was over, Wyatt immediately launched into apologies, "Shit, I'm *so* sorry! I couldn't stop in time, I— Fuck, I feel horrible. Let me get a towel or something."

But then, Andy cautiously opened his eyes and erupted into laughter, much to his surprise. "Jesus, I feel like I just got soaked with a firehouse." He turned to look at himself on the screen and started laughing even harder, "I look like a fucking glazed donut!"

Wyatt watched as some of his cum slid down Andy's face and dribbled between his legs onto his erection. Andy didn't seem to notice, but Wyatt's own cock jumped at the sight. He didn't understand why it would, though.

Despite still feeling mortified, Andy's laughter eventually got Wyatt chuckling, too. The group chat was a frenzy of messages simultaneously expressing amusement and arousal. Apparently, one straight roommate accidentally blowing a load on the face of another was a big hit with the fans.

Wyatt relaxed a bit, but apologized again, "I'm sorry, man."

Andy wiped his face clean with his t-shirt and shrugged, "It's fine. I'm more impressed than anything. That was a fuckton of jizz, dude."

"Yeah," Wyatt looked away bashfully. "Sorry for getting some in your mouth."

Andy blushed a little bit, but playfully smacked his lips together and joked, "You know, I'll be honest, the lube was actually worse. Let's not make a habit of it, though."

"Agreed," Wyatt laughed, trying to seem as laid-back as Andy was. In reality, though, his mind was racing through a million different thoughts. He was still grappling with the fact that Andy had even touched his hard cock, never mind the fact that he'd made him come. How would he ever be able to look his best friend in the eye again without remembering that he'd given him an orgasm? More than that, how would he ever be able to look him in the eye again knowing that he had, in fact, given him the best handjob of his life?

Chapter Seven

The rest of the live stream had gone well. Andy had gotten off shortly after Wyatt did (though, he did not shoot his wad on anyone's face), and it had turned out to be his most popular stream to date. After the recording had been posted to his timeline, there was a massive influx of new subscribers. They'd gotten three thousand signups in the first two hours after the stream. Andy had been hoping for a little bump in traffic after the show, but this far exceeded his expectations. It was clear that everyone was a *very* big fan of Wyatt and that they liked seeing the two of them together.

Andy wanted to celebrate the success of their first stream with beers and some video games, but Wyatt was acting weird after the show. He mumbled that he was tired and spent most of the day alone in his room. Andy was confused by this at first. After all, the show had gone so well. Why was he being weird? Was it the whole jizzing on his face thing? Because if anyone should be feeling weird about that it was him, not Wyatt.

Then, Andy remembered what his first stream felt like. He was nervous and exposed and utterly vulnerable. In all honesty, he felt dirty. To cope with it, he'd taken a long shower and spent most of the day in bed watching movies on his laptop. It only made sense that Wyatt was going through something similar now. In time, the inherent shame around nakedness would go away, and he would realize that it wasn't a big deal. That's how it had been for him.

Andy had become infinitely more comfortable with his body and sexuality since starting FanFrenzy. The idea of ass play had been inconceivable to him before then, but now it was something he did often without a second thought. In fact, it was probably this newfound comfort with sex that made swallowing some of Wyatt's cum tolerable. Old Andy definitely would've had a meltdown about something like that. But New Andy was far more enlightened. He understood that FanFrenzy was a job, just like anything else, and while some people dealt with bullshit at their jobs every single day, others dealt with jizz. *C'est la vie.*

On top of that, it turned out that sperm *did* taste better than lube, surprisingly. And while Andy didn't particularly care for his own brand (yes, he had tasted himself before; it's like Wyatt said, What guy hasn't?), Wyatt's cum tasted sweeter than he expected. Still salty, sure. But not unpleasant.

Andy caught himself wondering if all guys tasted different and decided that it probably wasn't something he should spend much mental energy on.

When evening rolled around, Wyatt finally came out of his room and approached Andy with a serious face. "Why need to talk."

Andy, who had just finished gawking at his FanFrenzy financial report since getting all of the new subscribers, felt his heart sink. He immediately assumed the worst.

They took a seat on the couch and Wyatt turned to him, determination in his eye. "We can't keep doing this forever."

Andy blinked. "What are you talking about? You've only done *one* show."

"No, I know. But we need a *plan*. I don't want to be getting naked in front of strangers for the next fifteen years of my life. I know that your spreadsheets show us retiring before we're thirty, but if we're actually going to pull that off then we need a strategy to draw new fans in and keep existing ones interested."

"Oh!" This was a surprise. After locking himself in his room all day, Andy thought that planning future shows would be the last thing Wyatt wanted to talk about. "Well, I think you're right. I mean, we can probably get away with jerking off for a while, but we're eventually going to have to dial things up."

"Right," Wyatt shifted uncomfortably. "So, I think we should talk about what that actually looks like."

"Okay, well I think a good place to start is to tell me what you're comfortable with, and then we'll go from there."

He shook his head. "I don't even know what the fans would want to see from us in the first place. Why don't you throw out ideas and I'll say yes or no?"

"Alright." Andy thought on this for a minute and decided to start easy. "The other day you say you were a 'maybe' on whether or not you'd jerk me off. What about now?"

Wyatt's face was tight, but he nodded. "Yeah, I would do it."

"Okay, Would you let me give you a blowjob?"

He grimaced. "Would you *want* to give me a blowjob?"

Andy rolled his eyes, "It doesn't matter what *I* want! We're doing this for the fans. And yes, I'd be willing to go down on you again in the future."

"Then, I guess I'm okay with it, too," he said, pinking slightly.

"Alright. Would you ever give me a blowjob?"

He chewed on his lip, debating his answer. Finally, he said, "Maybe, but not right away. I'd need some time to work up to that if I was going to do it."

"Fair enough. Would you kiss me?"

The flush in his cheeks deepened. "What kind of kiss?"

Again, Andy rolled his eyes. "Butterfly," he deadpanned. "Dude, what kind of kissing do you *think* I mean!? People wanna see tongue-on-tongue action! So, are you willing to give it to me French or not?"

Now as red as a beet, Wyatt buried his face into his hands. "God, I don't know! …Maybe?"

Andy sighed and pulled Wyatt's hands away and cupped his face with his own.

Wyatt's eyes went wide. "You're not about to kiss me now, are you?"

"No," he said. "I just need you to look at me and listen while I put things into perspective for you, okay? I jerked you off today. I put my mouth on your dick. I tasted your cum. And you watched me shoot a load onto my chest. Don't you think we're beyond the point of being squeamish about kissing?"

Wyatt thought on this for a moment and said, "Yeah, probably. But doesn't kissing feel more intimate than that other stuff?"

"Maybe," he shrugged. He hadn't considered that before. "I'll be honest, though, choking on your dick felt pretty intimate."

Wyatt snorted despite himself. "Yeah, that's valid. If you can do that, I'm sure I can deal with some kissing."

"If it makes you feel any better, we can put that at the end of the list, right alongside you giving me a blowjob."

"Thanks, but we still don't have much to do leading up to that."

"Right. Let's throw around more ideas." Andy stroked his chin thoughtfully. "How about me giving you a facial?"

Wyatt took a breath but nodded. "Yes. But not in the mouth."

"Coward."

"Shut up."

"What about frotting?"

"What's that?"

"Like sliding our dicks together."

"Oh. Yeah, I guess that's fine, too."

"What about fingering?"

Wyatt paused. "Who's fingering who?"

"Who's fingering *whom*," Andy corrected.

"God, you're a nightmare. Just answer the question."

"Well, given that you're having me make the distinction, I take that to mean you're not interested in volunteering. So, I suppose you'll be fingering me."

"Yeah, I'd prefer that."

"So that's a yes?"

"I guess so."

Huh. Andy was surprised that Wyatt sooner finger his ass than kiss him. They evidently had different opinions about which acts were more intimate. Not that Andy minded getting fingered, of course. Though, it occurred to him that Wyatt would be the first person ever (himself excluded) to be inside of him like that. The idea of his strong fingers sliding into his ass and massaging his sweet spot made his dick twitch in his shorts. But it was only because he had trained his dick to get hard every time he did butt stuff. It definitely had nothing to do with *who* would be playing with his butt.

Another idea came to him then, and without thinking, he asked, "Would you fuck me?" Wyatt's eyes flew open with shock, and Andy immediately backpedaled, "With my dildo I mean!

"Oh…" Wyatt cleared his throat and shifted his weight on the couch cushion. "Um, yeah. Sure."

An awkward stretch of silence passed between them, an unspoken question hanging in the air. Andy picked at the hem of his shirt, and Wyatt took an interest in his fingernails.

Then, they turned to each other at the same time and began talking simultaneously:

"We shouldn't, should we?"

"That would be crazy, right?"

They answered simultaneously, too:

"Nah, probably not."

"Definitely crazy."

The awkward silence returned, and they sat together fidgeting for another painful minute. Andy chewed on his lip, trying to figure out how he truly felt about the idea of Wyatt fucking him. His knee-jerk reaction was to say *Hell no!* But when he stopped and thought about it, he began questioning if it would really be that bad. After all, he'd taken a sizable dildo up the ass and enjoyed it. Would it be so different? And he was fantasizing more and more about getting pegged. This was practically the same thing, right? Also, he trusted Wyatt, and he definitely wanted his first time to be with someone he trusted.

God, this was crazy. This whole train of thought was completely ridiculous! The idea of him and Wyatt *fucking*? No way. He could make his peace with blowjobs and cum guzzling, but getting fucked was simply too much.

Still… The idea rolled over in his mind again and again, and he continued to worry at his lip.

Finally, he said, "But if we end up doing this FanFrenzy thing long enough—"

Wyatt quickly finished the thought, "Then we'll probably have to pull out the big guns eventually."

"Right! And I'd say that's the biggest gun in our arsenal."

"Without a doubt. So, it's definitely at the very end of the list, past blowjobs and kissing and everything else."

"One hundred percent. I mean, there's a good chance we would never even have to go that far."

"Exactly. It's just there in case of emergencies."

"For sure. And it wouldn't have to be a big deal either."

"Not at all. 'Cause this is just a job."

"And we're best friends."

"And we're doing this for our financial freedom."

"Right."

"Exactly."

"For sure."

"Yep."

They stared at each for a moment before both looking away uneasily. Then, Andy cleared his throat.

"Maybe that's enough strategizing for today."

"Yeah," Wyatt nodded feverishly. "Good call."

Andy stood up and hitched a thumb over his shoulder. "I'm gonna go to the bathroom." He didn't even have to go; he just needed an excuse to leave the room. As he made for his bedroom, Wyatt spoke.

"Wait, one more thing."

Andy turned and raised an eyebrow.

"I was thinking," he continued shyly, "if we're going to be doing this sex stuff with each other, we should probably be exclusive for the time being. I mean, if we were going on dates with other people and hooking up and stuff, it might be a headache to have to keep getting tested all the time."

Andy hadn't considered this before, but it made a certain amount of sense. If they were going to be sharing fluids on the reg, they needed to be safe. Exclusivity was an elegant solution to that problem. Besides, dating would probably be easier when their FanFrenzy days were behind them anyway. He didn't imagine many girls would be comfortable with the idea that he was regularly getting off with his roommate when they weren't around.

"That's a good idea," he said. Then, he walked over to Wyatt and held out his hand. "No other sexual partners."

They shook on it.

———

Alone in his room, after Wyatt had turned in for the night, Andy logged onto his FanFrenzy account to check on their current subscriber count. They had several hundred more than the last time he checked. At this rate, they were going to hit ten thousand before next weekend!

He clicked through some of the comments on the video upload from their show earlier. People seemed to really enjoy the addition of Wyatt to the channel, and their giddy anticipation for future content was positively palpable through the screen. Several users were speculating how far the two of them would go. Andy felt relieved that he and Wyatt had strategized earlier, as awkward as it was. They had a decent amount of ideas lined up that they could work through over the coming months to satisfy the fans.

As he continued scrolling, he saw that someone had reposted the gif of him failing miserably at giving Wyatt a blowjob. Another user had taken the gif, slowed it down, and zoomed in. Watching it, he was suddenly reminded of a viral video he'd seen years back of a seagull attempting to hork down an entire hotdog in one gulp.

He was mortified.

There was no way he was making an ass of himself like that again. If he was going down on Wyatt at some point in the future, then he needed to be prepared. He needed practice.

He swung his legs off the bed and went to his desk drawer to retrieve his dildo. Then, he sat cross-legged on his bed with his laptop and searched for a blowjob tutorial on PornHut. On the first page of results, he came across a video thumbnail with a modestly dressed woman holding a banana. He clicked on it.

The video turned out to be surprisingly educational. In fact, it didn't seem like porn at all. The woman stayed dressed and didn't even demonstrate on the banana. She simply stood in front of a green screen and walked the viewer through the best practices of giving good head using bullet points and oddly scientific illustrations. She didn't even call it a blowjob. She said *fellatio* instead.

Andy watched the video all the way through, taking mental notes. Relax the throat and tongue, breathe through the nose, avoid using teeth, inch down a little at a time, and know thy limits. Seemed simple enough.

"And remember," the woman said, smiling into the camera, "practice makes perfect." Then, she waved, and the video ended.

Out of curiosity, Andy scrolled down to the comments section. The top comment was posted two years ago, and it said:

This video helped me SO much!! I followed the instructions and after a couple weeks of practice I was finally able to deepthroat my boyfriend! The tips in the vid are simple but they REALLY WORK. Thank you so much!! My bf thanks you too ;)

Well, results don't lie, right? The only thing left for Andy to do now was actually practice. So, he grabbed his dildo and brought the tip of it to his mouth. He hesitated for a moment. This felt ridiculous. But he was adamant about improving his skills. He quietly vowed to himself that there would be no more embarrassing blowjob gifs of him online.

He stuck his tongue out and gave it a little lick. Bleh. It tasted gross, like chemicals. An actual dick probably tasted better (one that wasn't covered in lube, of course). But the flavor didn't deter him. He licked his lips and then wrapped his mouth around the tip. So far so good. He inched down bit by bit, continuously reminding himself to keep the muscles in his throat relaxed. Without any trouble at all, he managed to get halfway down.

This was easier than he thought. If he hadn't shoved the entirety of Wyatt's dick in his mouth in one go, he probably would've lasted considerably longer than he did. He might've even gotten him off that way. The fans would've loved that. Next time, he wouldn't disappoint.

Feeling encouraged by his progress, he bobbed further down the length of the dildo. He was nearing the back of his throat now, and his body's natural instinct was to cough the foreign object out. He pulled it out once to clear the tickle in his throat, but then returned to his task with determination. Per the video's guidance, he breathed through his nose and kept his muscles relaxed. Amazingly, he was able to take it farther this time.

He kept this up for several minutes, inching further down the fake cock while being ever-mindful of his teeth. His eyes closed as he found a rhythm, and he experimented with different amounts of suction and the tightness of his lips. He found that imagining a real dick in his mouth helped him to be more considerate of his actions. After all, the whole point of this was to make someone else feel good.

Of course, being that the only dick he had ever had in his mouth before was Wyatt's, that was ultimately who he thought about. He recalled the noises that Wyatt had made earlier when he was stroking him, and his dick started to plump in his basketball shorts. Then, he remembered the taste of him, the salty-sweet cum that had landed in his mouth. He imagined what it might be like to take Wyatt's full load in his mouth. The thought didn't repulse him. On the contrary, his cock was fully hard now.

Thoroughly lost in the moment, Andy moaned without realizing it. His dick strained against the fabric of his shorts, and he began moving his hips in search of friction. He was taking the full length of the dildo now, all the way down to the fake balls. It wasn't something he'd ever thought could be psychologically arousing, but the idea of having someone else in his throat was surprisingly hot. It made him feel powerful in an odd way.

When it became apparent that he was going to blow a load in his shorts if he didn't stop, the reality of the situation struck him. He was imagining Wyatt while deepthroating a dildo, remembering the taste of his cum on his tongue, and it was turning him on. More than that, it was going to get him off.

The realization snapped him out of his cock-sucking flow state, and his throat tightened. He pulled the dildo out, sputtering and coughing just like he had earlier during the live stream. But he didn't feel embarrassed about his failed attempt this time—on the contrary, he knew now that he *was* capable of giving a decent blowjob. Instead, he was embarrassed by his body's response to his own imagination. This little experiment should not have been such a turn-on to him.

Maybe he had just gone too long without sex. That was probably it. Of course, getting laid was currently out of the question. He and Wyatt had only just agreed to exclusivity a couple of hours ago.

Andy sighed and put away his sex toy, his boner finally beginning to soften. *This is all just temporary*, he reminded himself. *And it'll all be worth it in the end.*

I   hope.

Chapter Eight

When the work week started, Wyatt walked into the office with a spring in his step. He almost didn't care about the performance improvement plan because he had taken the first steps to get himself out of this hellhole job. He was still a ways off from actually quitting—he needed to be sure this FanFrenzy thing was sustainable and not just a one-off stroke of luck—but the idea that he could walk away from this shitty office someday in the near future and never return was enough to keep his spirits bright. Optimism carried him swiftly through the day.

The uneasiness he felt after the live stream had gone away thanks to a good night's sleep. With a rested mind, he realized that it was silly to feel awkward about enjoying the handjob Andy had given him. Someone was stroking his dick—of course he enjoyed it! It wasn't rocket science, and it certainly didn't deserve overthinking. At the end of the day, Andy was right—this FanFrenzy thing was just a job like anything else. And since this job entailed having regular orgasms, Wyatt figured that he might as well allow himself to enjoy them. There was no point in feeling shame about it. Andy didn't seem to, so why should he?

On his drive home from work that evening, Wyatt was thinking about other strategies they could implement to keep their fans engaged throughout the week. He and Andy had decided to keep their live streams to the weekends for the time being since his day job robbed him of most of his energy. Starting a live stream after having worked an eight-hour shift did not seem ideal. Still, that didn't mean that they couldn't post teaser videos and pics on the weekdays to keep people interested. He had a few ideas in mind that he was eager to share with Andy.

When he got to their apartment, it was clear that Andy had FanFrenzy on his mind, too, because he greeted him at the door with his laptop in hand.

"Check it out, dude!" he said excitedly. "We've got over ninety-five hundred fans now! The response from the stream we did has been insane. Everyone's excited to see what happens next."

Wyatt mentally calculated how much their monthly income was at that rate, and then a thought occurred to him. "Wait, how do taxes work for FanFrenzy?

Andy blinked. "What do you mean?"

"Like what kind of tax form do they send you?"

He shrugged sheepishly. "I dunno. I haven't been doing this for very long, remember? Why?"

"Because we might need to manage our own deductions." Andy gave him a worried, confused look, and he waved a pacifying hand. "On second thought, don't worry about it. I'll handle the finance stuff.

"Thank God. I'd be lost without you, dude."

Wyatt dropped onto the couch, "I've been thinking that we should take some videos or photos to post throughout the week to hold people over until the weekend."

"That's a good idea," Andy took a seat beside him. "What did you have in mind?"

"Maybe you could take some stealthy videos of me showering or something. Or maybe I have an accidental dick

161

slip while sitting on the couch and you take photos without me noticing. Something candid and seemingly spontaneous. Kind of like your old content."

Andy's eyes went wide. "How do you know about my old content?"

"I signed up for a thirty-day subscription," he said. Andy stared at him in disbelief. He simply shrugged, "I was curious. Anyway, I think the whole 'sneaky roommate' thing would still hold some appeal with fans. We can carve out a few hours to film some stuff and then post it over the coming weeks. People don't have to know they were staged."

"Alright, I'm down," he said. "Honestly, they can't seem to get enough of you. I've been getting so many DMs asking if you'll be coming back for the next stream. Maybe these videos will give them their fix of Jack."

Wyatt blushed slightly at hearing how popular he was with the crowd. "Awesome, then let's do it."

After dinner, they spent a couple of hours filming "candid" videos of Wyatt. For one of them, Andy filmed through the crack in Wyatt's slightly ajar bedroom door as he stripped out of his work clothes to put on leisurewear. Wyatt, of course, made sure to angle himself in a way that

162

his butt was perfect in the shot as he bent over to grab his clothes off the floor. They had to film it twice because his bedroom had been too dark the first time. So, they turned on the overhead lights and his bedside lamp, reset the scene, and got it on the second take.

In another video, Wyatt was laying on the couch watching TV with one leg propped up so the baggy leg of his gym shorts slid down and revealed a glimpse of his cock and balls. In this video, Andy was in the kitchen and pretending to make a snack while secretly filming and zooming in on his package. Wyatt, who was absorbed with the movie, was seemingly oblivious to the camera.

For the last video of the night, Andy was supposed to sneak into Wyatt's room while he was taking a shower and film him. They decided that Wyatt would "catch" Andy in the act this time and pretend to get mad before throwing his towel at the camera.

So, Wyatt hopped into the shower, leaving his bathroom door open and his bedroom door conveniently unlocked, and waited for Andy to silently sneak in and start recording him. As he showered off, he amusedly thought that this setup felt like a Hitchcock movie. Or at least a Hitchcock porn parody. Had that been done before? Probably.

A few minutes later, he saw a shape emerge in the doorway of his bathroom from the corner of his eye. He very deliberately didn't look in that direction and continued to rinse himself clean, hoping silently that Andy was able to get decent footage of him through the steamy clear-plastic shower curtains. Then, he turned off the water, grabbed his towel, and patted himself dry. Everything was going according to plan so far, and he reminded himself to act surprised when he pulled back the curtain and saw the camera.

Little did Wyatt know that before starting the recording, Andy had gone into his closet, pulled down his terrifying latex clown mask from last Halloween, and slipped it over his head. When Wyatt stepped out of the tub and looked up at Andy, he let out a loud, startled yelp.

"*SHIT! JESUS CHRIST!*" Wyatt didn't have to *act* surprised, and he also didn't have to act pissed. He balled up his towel and pelted it at Andy whose mad giggling was muffled by the sound of his mask. "Come here, Andrew!"

He bolted after him, and Andy turned to run, laughter suddenly mixing with panic, "*Oh, shit!*"

Wyatt tackled him to his bed, not even caring that he was buck naked and still damp. They rolled around and tussled all the while laughing like schoolboys.

"Bleh! You're getting me all wet!"

"Serves you right!"

Eventually, Wyatt got the upper hand and pulled the mask off, chucking it across the room. Then, he rolled Andy onto his back, straddled his hips, and pinned his shoulders down. He leaned over him, faces just inches apart. They stared at each other, panting and giggling and pink in the face.

"I fucking hate you, dude," Wyatt laughed.

"Oh, come on, it was funny," Andy protested with a smile.

"Mark my words, I'll have my revenge."

"Oh yeah? What are you gonna do?"

"I don't know yet. Probably teabag you in your sleep or something."

Andy gave him a funny smile and his cheeks went a shade darker. "Well, uh, you're kind of already teabagging my belly button right now."

Wyatt looked down between their bodies to see that Andy's shirt had ridden up during the scuffle and that his

165

freshly-showered cock and balls were sitting directly on his exposed belly.

"Oh, oops. Sorry…" He leaned back but doing so meant that his naked ass was now sitting on Andy's crotch. Through the thin fabric of Andy's basketball shorts, he could feel the gentle mound of his dick nestled against his crack. This was far more intimate than it needed to be, and Andy clearly thought so too because a small look of surprise flashed through his eyes.

Wyatt cleared his throat and scrambled off the bed to retrieve his towel. Andy got up too, trying to play it cool, and picked up his phone which had fallen to the carpet when Wyatt tackled him. As Wyatt threw on his pajamas, Andy rewatched the video and started laughing.

"Dude, the look on your face is priceless. I can't *wait* to post this."

Wyatt sidled up beside him, and Andy replayed it for him. He hated to admit it, but it *was* pretty funny. The terror in his eyes was certainly genuine. Nobody would suspect that this was a staged video.

"God, I hope this doesn't go viral," he groaned.

Andy grinned mischievously, "I hope it *does* go viral."

Wyatt rolled his eyes and picked up the clown mask from the floor, shoving it into Andy's arms. "You better sleep with one eye open tonight, you little shit."

Chapter Nine

"So, he said yes?" Astonishment was written all over Leslie's face.

"Yep," Andy said, trying to sound as casual as he could while doing leg presses. "We had our first show together over the weekend."

"No shit?" She paused and seemed to chew on this information, looking thoughtful. "What was that like?"

"Eh, it was okay." He puffed out a few short breaths. "Kind of made an ass of myself, though."

"Well, that's not surprising," she smirked, earning her a dirty look.

He finished with his last two reps then locked the press into place and slid out of the chair. "Well, everything had been going fine until someone donated a bunch of money to see me blow him."

Her mouth fell open. "Oh my God, tell me you did not actually suck your best friend's dick during his very first show."

"…

"*Dude.*

He folded his arms defensively. "What!? Why is that such a bad thing?"

"Have you even sucked dick before?"

"Well, no…"

"I rest my case."

"It wasn't that bad!" he protested, feeling his cheeks burn. Then, he hesitated and thought back to the incident. "Okay. It was pretty bad, but it only lasted for like half a second."

She fell quiet and narrowed her eyes at him warily. "Why? What happened? You didn't barf on the poor guy, did you?"

"God, no! I just—" He rubbed a hand over his face. "I just sorta dove headfirst onto it without thinking and nearly choked myself. I coughed my head off for like five minutes afterward.

She cringed "And this show was happening *live*?"

He nodded.

"Jesus, Andy, I'm getting secondhand embarrassment just listening to this story. You can't just shove a dick down your throat right out of the gate and expect it to go well. There's an art to giving a good blowjob."

"Well, I know that *now*! I've done some research since then and started practicing."

She raised an eyebrow. "Practicing?

"Yeah, on a…toy that I have."

"I see. And how has that been going for you?"

"Pretty well actually!" He perked up. He'd been wanting to tell someone about his blowjob progress, but there was no one he could confide in. He didn't want to tell Wyatt because he wanted his new skills to be a surprise. "I've gotten pretty good at deepthroating. I'm kinda proud, not gonna lie."

She gave him an approving look, "Wow, deepthroating already? You sound like a natural."

"I wouldn't say that," he said modestly. "I just followed a tutorial I found online and noticed an improvement right away. Although, I'm still not one hundred percent sure I'm doing it right, because I've been getting a scratchy throat lately."

"That's normal," she said. "Warm tea and honey always helps me."

Andy smiled, "Thanks for the tip! I'll definitely try that."

She stared at him for a moment with a faint smile playing on her mouth. "You seem pretty determined to improve your dick-sucking skills."

He shrugged, "Well, yeah. This is my job. I want to be good at what I do. Nobody's gonna pay to watch a shitty blowjob."

"That's a fair point." She thought about this for a moment and said, "What are you doing with your hands?"

He frowned and glanced down at his palms, confused. "What do you mean?"

"I mean, there's more to a good blowjob than just sticking a dick in your mouth. Hands can take your head game to the next level, so make sure you're using them."

Andy's eyes widened in awe as if she'd just shared a secret of the universe. He hadn't considered that before now, but when he thought back on his sexual encounters, the most memorable blowjobs he'd received *did* have a fair bit of hand action. How could he have overlooked something so obvious?

"Oh my God, I didn't even think about that," he said excitedly. "So, what should I do with them?" He gave her his undivided attention as if he expected to be quizzed on this subject someday.

She gave him a dry look, "I'm not here to coach you on blowjob techniques.

"Oh, come on! You obviously have more experience with this sort of thing than I do. *Pleeease.*"

She was unfazed by his puppy-dog eyes. "You're a smart guy, Andy. You can figure it out on your own. Besides, different guys like different things, so there's no 'right' way to do it anyway. You've just got to try stuff and see what your guy likes. Get creative."

The words *your guy* did something weird to Andy's insides. Wyatt wasn't *his* guy. He didn't *have* a guy at all. And yet, all of the research and practice he'd been putting into his dick-sucking skills as of late would ultimately benefit Wyatt more than anyone else. Yes, it was true that he didn't want to make a fool of himself on camera again, but he also had to admit that his recent obsession with giving, not just adequate, but *good* head, stemmed from a desire to impress Wyatt. But why?

Because Wyatt is my best friend, he thought, *and if he has to suffer through this FanFrenzy thing—which was all MY idea—then the least I can do is try to make it somewhat enjoyable. It's as simple as that.*

But that answer didn't completely satisfy the doubt lingering in his mind. Even so, it would have to be good enough for the time being, because he didn't want to think about it anymore. He pushed the thoughts far away where he wouldn't have to deal with them again.

Suddenly sober, he cleared his throat and nodded to Leslie, "Thanks for the advice. I'll try the tea and honey thing." Then, he slid back into the chair of the leg press machine and started his next set.

She watched him with a hint of curiosity and concern in her eyes, but he didn't notice.

———

They recorded their second show a week after the first. Andy had uploaded the video of Wyatt undressing in his room on Thursday and it had been a hit with the fans. Then

173

on Friday, he made a written post on his page informing everyone that Jack would be returning for the next show. The news was met with a lot of excitement, and the stream ended up having the highest turnout of attendees to date.

Despite the bigger audience, Wyatt seemed more at ease the second time around. Which was a relief. Andy saw it as a sign that he was warming up to the job. Of course, for the sake of the fans, he still acted the part of nervous, inexperienced straight guy who was only begrudgingly going along with everything. Which wasn't a total lie. He *was* an inexperienced straight guy, and despite his improved comfort levels, there were still moments when genuine uncertainty flashed through his eyes. Like when they immediately hit their new tip goals just like last weekend.

The plan had, once again, been to gradually ease Wyatt into the lasted sexual acts they had planned out. Today, they were supposed to start off easy, getting naked after the first goal was met and then getting hard after the second. When they reached the third goal, Wyatt would then stroke Andy, and when the fourth and final one was reached, he would jerk them both off at the same time to completion. It had taken some convincing to get Wyatt to agree to the final goal. He thought it was "too soon" for their dicks to touch.

But Andy argued that it was just a fancy version of a handjob and one of the tamest things on their list.

Andy should've known that things would play out exactly the same as last time. The fans were *hungry* to see them together. They surpassed all four tip goals before they'd had the chance to get their shirts off.

"You guys are insane," Andy laughed, marveling at the screen.

Wyatt laughed, too, but it sounded strained. That was when Andy saw a flicker of nervousness on his face. He made a mental note to make the tip goals higher next time. Maybe that would give them the chance to take things a bit slower.

Then, the visible nerves were replaced with a look of determination, and Wyatt reached for the bottle of lube. "Alright, let's do this."

Fully naked now, Andy and Wyatt inched closer together. As Wyatt was pouring lube into his palm, Andy— who had gotten himself halfway hard already—noticed that Wyatt was still very flaccid. There was no way frottage was going to work like that, so he reached out and took him into his hand. Wyatt tensed, clearly surprised, but then after a moment he relaxed and let him continue. Andy didn't see the harm in giving him a hand. Thanks to his time spent cam modeling, he could practically get hard on command these days, but this was all still new to Wyatt so it only made sense that he needed a bit of help. And it seemed to do the trick. Wyatt was thickening in his hand quickly.

Just before Wyatt closed the cap on the lube, Andy stopped jerking him and held out his hand. Without a word, Wyatt poured some into his palm and then snapped the bottle shut. Andy returned his attention to Wyatt's cock, working the lube along his length. He was almost completely hard now.

Wyatt hesitated only for a second before reaching out and grabbing Andy's dick. Andy let out a little gasp when one of his broad, strong hands wrapped around his shaft. It was at that moment he realized how long it had been since someone else had touched *him*. The warm touch of another person, of Wyatt, felt amazing.

They stood together, jerking each other, as Wyatt eventually got a handle on things (no pun intended). He quickly became more confident—probably realizing that stroking another dude's dick was not all that different from stroking his own—and was soon giving Andy one of the better handjobs he'd received in his life.

Andy closed his eyes as Wyatt twisted his fist around his head in small circles, and a very audible moan escaped his mouth. The sound surprised him, and he started, blinking at Wyatt as his face went hot. Wyatt raised an eyebrow, looking both amused and smug.

Andy bashfully turned away, focusing his attention on the group chat. He rolled his eyes at the recent messages.

Having a moment, Ace? ;)

Omg he's SO into it xD

LOL Jack looks so pleased with himself

Not that this isn't hot but I'm ready to see y'all touch dicks lmfao

He gave Wyatt a questioning look as if to ask, *Ready?* Wyatt nodded, and they shuffled nearer, lining themselves up so that their dicks pressed together. It became immediately apparent to Andy that this idea was better on paper. He hadn't considered the logistics before now. They were *very* close. Practically nose-to-nose. Also, Wyatt was a

177

couple of inches taller than he was, so he had to bend his knees to get on his level.

Andy thought he was beyond this point of cam modeling awkwardness, but evidently, he wasn't the unshakable porn veteran he thought he was. What the hell was he supposed to do with his hands? He envied Wyatt for having a job to do. Standing there, doing fuck all with his arms hanging limply at his sides, was awkward as hell.

But then Wyatt wrapped a large hand around both of their cocks, stroking them, and Andy's discomfort and stiffness started to give way to pleasure. The sensation of Wyatt's cock pressed against the underside of his own was intense. He stared down in awe at Wyatt's hand, griping and working them both in one fluid motion. There was something obscene about seeing their dicks pressed together like that, and it ignited a lustful fire in Andy's belly.

Another moan escaped him as his hips began moving on their own accord, thrusting into Wyatt's fist. Wyatt let out a low groan of his own, and Andy looked up to meet his eyes. A deep flush spread across the bridge of Wyatt's nose and his mouth hung open slightly. The dark hunger brewing behind his heavy eyelids told Andy that he was enjoying this just as much as he was, so he rocked his hips more

178

enthusiastically. Wyatt bit down on his bottom lip, another throaty sound rolled out of him.

Fuck, it felt good. Infinitely better than just a run-of-the-mill handjob. One of Andy's hands found Wyatt's waist to keep himself steady as he continued to rut against him. Wyatt either didn't notice or simply didn't care.

Andy was personally beyond the point of caring about how much he was enjoying this. The perfect slickness of Wyatt's cock gliding along his was incredible. Nothing else mattered. The group chat was a faraway thought, as irrelevant as what the neighbors were having for dinner tonight. He was living fully in the present, tuned in solely to the connection of their bodies and the pressure building inside him.

His head fell forward, resting in the crook of Wyatt's neck as he continued thrusting vigorously into his grip, panting hot breath over his collarbone. A whine rose from Andy's throat, a helpless, pleading sound

Wyatt's low voice rumbled through him like distant thunder. "Do it," he breathed. "Come for me."

Those words pushed him over the edge and his orgasm tore through him like a bolt of lightning. He jerked wildly against Wyatt, unleashing his hot load onto both of their bodies.

Once the aftershock finished echoing through him and he was no longer afraid of his wobbly legs giving out, he drew back from the heat of Wyatt's shoulder and looked up at him. His blue eyes looked like the sea after a storm. There was uncertainty in them, a quiet acknowledgment that something unplanned had happened between them, but there was also the faint twinkle of a smile.

"How was that?" He asked softly.

Andy breathed out a shaky laugh. "Holy fuck, dude. That was…" He glanced down between them at the mess he'd made. There was so much cum. Had it all been him? He looked at Wyatt with a question in his eyes, "Did you also…?"

Wyatt chuckled and shook his head, "That's all you, dude."

He looked back down between them in disbelief. That might've been the biggest cumshot he'd ever had.

It occurred to him then that Wyatt hadn't gotten off yet. Rather than let him jerk himself off to finish the job, Andy wanted to repay Wyatt for the best orgasm he'd had in recent memory.

He dropped to his knees and looked up at Wyatt whose eyebrows had shot up to his hairline.

"Is this okay?" Andy asked.

Wyatt gave him a doubtful look, "Are you sure you want to after last time?"

He managed to fight back his smile. Wyatt had no idea what was coming. "I'm sure."

Wyatt shrugged as if to say *I think you're making a mistake bud,* but nodded at him regardless. Andy shifted forward and grabbed his cock. It was covered with his cum which he found hot in a filthy kind of way. He took him slowly into his mouth. Tasting himself on Wyatt made his own dick twitch and stoked the fires of desire inside him. He hummed around his shaft as he took him deeper.

Wyatt hummed in both pleasure and mild surprise, "Oh, fuck."

Andy took this as a sign of encouragement and proceeded to start jerking him with his fist as he bobbed further down. Wyatt was bigger than his dildo, but Andy was up for the challenge. He inched more and more of his thick cock into his throat until his nose finally met something solid, buried in the bush of Wyatt's furry pubes.

Wyatt gasped, and Andy drew back before taking him to the hilt again.

"My *God.*" Wyatt's words were ragged and thick.

Andy used his other hand to cup his heavy balls and felt Wyatt shudder. His strong thighs began to shake. A long, drawn-out moan fell out of his mouth, and his hips rocked forward slightly as if he was struggling to keep his balance. The feeling of Wyatt pushing his cock further down Andy's throat sent a thrill directly to his dick. The fire in him blazed. Using both of his hands, he reached around, grabbed Wyatt's ass, and rocked his hips forward again.

"*Fuck!*" Wyatt gasped.

Andy continued pulling him into his mouth, again and again. The sensation of Wyatt fucking his face made him rock hard. It was only just dawning on him that he apparently had a deepthroating kink. Who would've known? Some distant voice in his head wondered if this sort of thing was common for straight men or not, but the thought died away with the overwhelming bliss of Wyatt stretching him.

Wyatt was muttering a string of broken, unintelligible phrases, letting Andy drive his hips forward harder and harder. The taste of his precum filled Andy's mouth, and his thrusts became choppy.

Finally, he managed to find his words. "I-I'm close…"

Andy doubled down on his efforts, squeezing Wyatt's ass hard as he pulled him into his mouth faster and faster. Only a few strokes later, Wyatt groaned loudly and bucked forward hard, wrapping his hands around Andy's head and holding himself steady as he pumped hot spurts of cum down his throat. Andy could feel every pulse of Wyatt's cock.

Wyatt's breath was ragged, and his legs trembled like jelly.

"Holy fuck," he breathed. Taking a shaky step backward, he withdrew from Andy's mouth.

Andy looked up into Wyatt's wrecked face—blotchy with lust and pupils completely blown. He smiled at him, feeling a little smug, "How was that?

He let out a shaky, almost disbelieving laugh. "Where the hell did you learn *that*?"

Andy shrugged, "Internet."

Oh shit, speaking of the internet, he'd forgotten all about the group chat, a fact that quietly unnerved him. FanFrenzy was the entire reason they were even doing any of this stuff, so to forget about the group chat was to forget about their true purpose for getting off together.

Andy shook the thought from his head. He needed to focus on the chat he neglected. He glanced at the screen and skimmed the recent messages.

Turns out the fans hadn't minded being neglected.

They'd made an additional fifteen hundred dollars in tips.

Chapter Ten

The second show had been more intense than the first, but it didn't shake Wyatt as much as he thought it might've. He and Andy were amazingly okay afterward. There seemed to be an unspoken awareness between them that they had both given each other mind-blowing orgasms, but despite that, they were able to carry on as bros just the same. They still played video games together and watched movies and made dinner. Since it was obvious to Wyatt that their FanFrenzy antics were not having any adverse side effects on their friendship—and since they were attracting more and more subscribers every day—he had no hangups about carrying on with things.

Wyatt was, of course, still at his day job, but he had more money in his savings than ever before, and he was making considerable strides in paying off his student loans. Though Sue Ellen was still a thorn in his side, life was better than it had been in a long time.

Part of it was the knowledge that he could quit his job soon if things with FanFrenzy continued to do well. Another part of it was that he was getting sex regularly now. Granted, it was sex with Andy and done purely for the money. But it was still sex! It's like that say goes: Sex is like pizza—even when it's bad, it's still pretty good. Truth be told, though, the sex with Andy *wasn't* bad. At all, actually. It was fun and laid-back and enjoyable—as much as he hated to admit it, Andy gave shockingly good head. Being with him also felt naughty in a thrilling kind of way, like they were intentionally breaking the rules. And despite being constantly nudged further outside of his comfort zone each week, Wyatt found the journey into the unfamiliar easy with Andy by his side.

They'd fallen into a rhythm. During the week they would take more "candid" content to post to the channel and plan out what their tip goals would be for their upcoming shows. A few weeks ago, Andy had given Wyatt a facial which wasn't as bad as he expected (though, he avoided getting any in his mouth). For another show, Wyatt got a blowjob while playing video games which was just as hot as he imagined it would be, regardless if Andy was the one giving it to him.

Their viewership continued to rise, and shortly after passing sixteen thousand subscribers, Wyatt decided that it was time to quit his normal job. He strategically waited to give Sue Ellen the news on the final day of his performance improvement plan. Even though he knew he would be leaving the company soon, he worked diligently to satisfy her unreasonable demands so that she couldn't fire him. He didn't want to give her the satisfaction. He intended to leave on his terms.

For the past two months, he worked his ass off to make sure that all of the managers he processed payroll for delivered their timesheets on time. That usually meant hounding them relentlessly with reminder emails and phone calls for *days* until they complied. On one occasion, he physically made a trip to a different department on his lunch break and cornered one of them. He'd gotten very unpopular very quickly. But he didn't care, because it paid off in the end. For the first time ever, there had been no payroll complaints filed against him.

On the day that his PIP ended, Sue Ellen called him into her office. She sat behind her desk as if she were sitting on a cactus. Rigid, tense, and barely holding back expletives. It was evident she hadn't expected to lose this cruel little game she'd started and that admitting defeat physically pained her

She cleared her throat, looking down at a document in her hands. "No complaints," she said simply, lips pursed. The disappointment was clear in her voice. "You've passed your PIP."

Wyatt pretended to be surprised. "I did? Oh wow, that's such a relief," he smiled. Then, he looked at her with as much innocent sincerity as he could muster, "So, I did a good job?"

Words of praise were not in Sue Ellen's lexicon. She'd never once said anything positive or congratulatory to any of her employees. But Wyatt recognized that he had her cornered and wanted to watch her squirm. She deserved it. This petty little contest was her idea, so she had no one to blame but herself. Play stupid games, win stupid prizes

Her jowls twitched as she struggled to hold back a grimace. Finally, she drew tight lips back and bared her

188

teeth, trying and failing to pass it off as a grin. Her nod was almost imperceptible.

Wyatt beamed, "Thank you, Sue Ellen. That really means a lot." He took note of the vein that was starting to bulge down the center of her forehead. It took a considerable amount of effort to keep the smugness out of his smile. He stood up, unclipped the building badge from his belt loop, and tossed it onto her desk. "I quit."

Her eyes were wide with shock and indignation. "What do you mean you *quit*?" she snapped.

"I mean that, effective immediately, I no longer work here."

When she saw the cold truth in his eyes, she faltered, floundering to find words. "You— But it's— You can't do that!" she said finally, huffing and turning red in the face. "You have to give your two weeks' notice!"

"No, I don't," he said. "That's a courtesy, not a requirement."

"But the pay period had just passed! You know that everyone has to do their part to remedy complaints! Would you really walk out on your team?"

She'd been robbed of the opportunity to get rid of Wyatt on her terms, and it was obvious that she was now scrambling to regain any control that she could. The only reason she wanted him to stay was so that she could continue to make his life hell and have the satisfaction of firing him herself one day. It was pathetic. And it irked Wyatt that she pretended to care about the team at all. He knew with absolute certainty that if he'd gotten a single complaint over the course of his PIP, she would've fired him immediately and let the team pick up his workload while she dragged her feet to find a replacement.

He looked at her evenly. "That's not my problem anymore. If you're that concerned about the team, maybe you could try pulling your own weight for a change.

Her eyes flared with anger, and her lips puckered like she'd just eaten a lemon. She said nothing, only breathed hotly through flared nostrils. The vein on her forehead looked like might pop soon.

Wyatt made no effort to hide his smugness now. He smiled sweetly at her and said, "Go to hell, Sue Ellen."

Then he turned on his heel and walked out of her office, closing the door behind him. A second later, there was a loud *clang!* on the other side. It sounded like something heavy—probably a stapler—had been thrown at the back of the door. Wyatt smiled to himself and continued merrily toward the elevators.

As he passed the cubicles, one of his coworkers, Abby, stuck her head out and looked at him.

"What was that noise?" she asked glancing toward Sue Ellen's office

"She's just a little upset that I quit."

Abby's eyes widened. "You quit!? Are you serious?

"Afraid so," he said with a sympathetic smile.

"Oh, hell no," she said scrambling for her purse. "You were the only thing keeping me sane in this place. If you're gone, I'm gone."

"What are you doing?"

"Quitting, obviously," she said, threading an arm into her cardigan. "But I'm going to HR, not her."

"That's probably a smart move."

Another one of their coworkers, Kyle, stepped out of his cubicle and looked at them anxiously, "I'm coming, too."

———

In the end, three members of Sue Ellen's team of five quit that day. As proud as she was of her high turnover rate, she apparently didn't appreciate the unexpected mass exodus. One of the remaining team members texted Wyatt telling him that Sue Ellen had a meltdown when she found out from HR about Abby and Kyle. Allegedly, she chucked a fax machine across the office and had to be escorted out by security. She ended up getting temporarily suspended while the higher-ups made their final decision regarding appropriate disciplinary action. From the sound of it, things didn't look good for her future at the company.

Even if Sue Ellen was replaced by someone better (which was an extremely low bar), Wyatt wouldn't want to keep working there anyway, and Abby and Kyle were of the same opinion. Turned out that they'd both been looking for work elsewhere and had upcoming job interviews scheduled anyway.

To celebrate their escape from Sue Ellen, the three of them and Andy had gone out to dinner. Wyatt and Andy had already planned to do something special for the occasion and decided the more the merrier. Andy was such a natural socialite and made conversation easily with the newcomers. Wyatt swore that he could charm the hat off of the Pope.

Hanging out with Kyle and Abby outside of work had been nice. Away from the context of the office, Wyatt had a chance to see their personalities shine. Abby was absurdly funny, which Wyatt had already gotten a sense of while working with her but now she wasn't holding back. She had the table laughing throughout their entire meal. Kyle on the other hand was more reserved but very kind and thoughtful and seemed to know a little bit about absolutely everything. The two of them naturally gravitated towards each other—Abby finding his little factoids genuinely interesting, and Kyle finding her laugh-out-loud hilarious.

After food and drinks, they all went to a dance club a couple of blocks away that Abby swore by. It turned out to be a blast.

It had been over a year since Wyatt had last been out dancing, and he forgot how much he missed losing himself in the music and strobing lights. The four of them danced as a group until Kyle and Abby gradually broke away and started dancing together. Wyatt looked over at them at one point and was surprised to see them kissing. Had they always been into each other? He wasn't sure, but it was sorta sweet seeing them like that. They'd always gotten along well as friends in the office, and Wyatt firmly believed romance should start with a healthy friendship. Amid the fuzzy haze of his fifth drink, he thought to himself absently that he wanted to find that for himself. A friendship that evolved naturally into love.

He reminded himself that it made no sense to think about relationships right now. He and Andy were committed to their retirement plan, and until they ended their porn careers, they were exclusive with each other. And maybe, he thought, that wasn't such a terrible thing. Andy was his favorite person in the world after all. He liked spending time with him, and they were having fun together. Besides, he was still young; there was more than enough time to find love later.

He focused his attention back on Andy who was dancing in front of him. He was smiling wide, yelling out the lyrics of the song while he shook his hips. His eyes were closed, his brown hair was plastered to his forehead, and an alcohol-induced flush stretched from one cheek to the other. The sight of him pulled at something inside Wyatt. At that moment, he felt so ridiculously lucky to have met him. Life without Andy was completely unimaginable. It made his chest ache to think that someday, when they were both older and married to their future wives, they wouldn't be living together anymore.

Would they live close to each other? What if they were both too busy with their families to hang out together? If they did hang out, would their wives always have to join them? What if he wanted to hang out with Andy one-on-one like old times?

Jesus, the gin and tonic had been a bad call. Gin had a way of making him introspective. All he wanted to do was enjoy the moment right now. To be with Andy and dance his cares away, to celebrate his escape from Sue Ellen and focus on the exciting road ahead.

He glanced over at Kyle and Abby again. They were still lip-locked, oblivious to the world around them.

"They're cute," Andy said over the music.

Wyatt turned to him—Andy was looking at them warmly. He was so damn *sincere*. Andy was the kind of person who was genuinely happy seeing other people happy, even people he didn't know. Wyatt smiled affectionately at him. Andy had such a good heart. It was one of the things Wyatt loved most about him.

Andy had leaned in close to him so that he could be heard over the sound of the club, and Wyatt could smell the pleasant mix of his cologne, laundry detergent, and natural musk. It was familiar and reminded him of their home. He leaned in slightly closer.

When Andy finally turned back and faced Wyatt, they were inches apart. Their eyes locked together. Something about Andy's familiar hazel eyes captured his attention. He'd seen them a thousand times before, but there was something new in them. Something magnetic. They were lidded and simmering with a dark curiosity that rendered Wyatt mute. He could only look back at those beautiful eyes and feel the pull between their bodies draw him closer.

Andy wet his lips with his tongue, and Wyatt followed the movement. He stared unapologetically at his mouth, soft and pink, and wondered for an absurd moment what it tasted like.

His bleary thoughts drifted back to Kyle and Abby. They were friends… He and Andy were friends, too… Was it really so strange to kiss a friend? They'd done much worse for FanFrenzy, after all. And kissing could totally be a friendly gesture, right? He was pretty sure he'd read that it was the norm in some countries to kiss your friends. Or maybe that had been burping after meals… His brain was too fuzzy to remember right now. But what difference did it make? Andy was his best bro, and he was so kind and funny and sweet, and his lips looked so soft, and it would be so easy to just lean forward a little bit and close the gap between them...

They both inched nearer.

"*Thank you all for coming out tonight!*" a voice blared through the speakers. Wyatt and Andy both jumped and took an awkward step away from each other.

"*I've got one final song for you all,*" the DJ continued. "*So, get your asses on the dance floor and MOVE!*"

An 80's dance song that Wyatt only sort of recognized blasted through the speakers. Immediately, the crowd went wild, and Abby suddenly appeared with Kyle in tow.

"I *love* this song!" she yelled.

And then, they were all dancing in a group again. The strangeness from before seemed to be a distant memory to Andy because he was shaking his hips and singing along loudly, smiling like a maniac. That smile made Wyatt's chest feel light and fluttery. He didn't know what the feeling meant. Perhaps he'd had too much to drink.

Shoving the thought away, Wyatt closed his eyes and moved to the rhythm of the music, letting the good vibrations of the night wash over him. It had been ages since he'd felt this free.

He smiled. Quitting his job had been the best decision he'd ever made. And it was all thanks to Andy.

———

Back at the apartment, Wyatt and Andy flopped down onto the couch sipping glasses of water. They were sweaty and tired and sobering up, though still riding the high from the club.

After a long stretch of companionable silence, Andy finally said, "I'm so proud of you for quitting. You look happier than I've seen you in a long time."

Wyatt gave him a smile. "Thanks, man. Honestly, I *feel* happier than I have in a long time. Like a weight has been lifted off of my chest. And I owe it to you." He held out his glass to Andy who tapped it lightly with his own. "Thank you."

Andy blushed and looked away. "I'm sure FanFrenzy wasn't the most ideal way of making a getaway, but I'm glad I could help."

"It hasn't been so bad," Wyatt admitted, taking another sip. Then he laughed, "God, I can't wait to sleep in on

Monday. I have so much free time now. What do you do with yourself all day?"

"Go to the gym, play video games, go for walks sometimes, make lunch, check the fan page for DMs. It's pretty laid back."

"That sounds perfect," he smiled sleepily. "I can't believe I'm getting paid so much for so few hours of actual work."

Andy fell quiet again for a moment, staring at the condensation on his glass, before letting out a funny sort of laugh. It sounded thin somehow. "Let's hope we hit our financial goals soon so we don't have to go much further down our list of show ideas."

Wyatt cocked his head. "What do you mean?

Andy lifted a shoulder and tried to laugh again. "You know—so we don't have to do all those things you're dreading. Like kissing and stuff."

He snorted. The fact that he'd ever been so opposed to kissing Andy was ridiculous to him now. They'd done far more intimate things. Kissing was the absolute least of his worries.

"I don't think kissing is going to be a big deal," he said.

"Really?"

Wyatt shrugged. "After the things we've already done? I'm not worried. Are you?"

Andy hesitated, and Wyatt frowned.

"You're not having second thoughts now, are you?"

"No!" Andy said hastily. "It's just that I think that maybe you were right before. Kissing *is* pretty intimate. It might be awkward at first."

"I feel like you're overthinking it," Wyatt said. "But we can practice if you're that worried about it."

"Right now?

Wyatt shrugged again. "Why not?"

Andy chewed on his lip in thought before finally nodding. They shifted on the couch, meeting at the middle cushion. Andy's eyes were suddenly filled with that same magnetic curiosity from the club, and once again, Wyatt was transfixed by them. He felt his face go warm and he tried telling himself that this wasn't any more intimate than the other things they'd done together. Taking a steadying breath, he cupped a hand on Andy's cheek and leaned forward.

When their lips connected, an electric current shot down his spine and he shuddered. Andy shuddered, too. But they didn't break away. They waited only a moment—for a heartbeat or two—before moving their mouths together, opening themselves to the other, and allowing their tongues to meet. Andy was warm and soft and tasted vaguely of spiced rum. Wyatt hummed against him.

Andy absently balled up his fists into Wyatt's shirt, tugging him closer, and Wyatt put his other hand on Andy's waist. Their mouths moved hungrily, desperately, as if the world were ending in a matter of minutes. A small, needy sound escaped Andy's mouth and Wyatt swallowed it up.

They shifted backward on the couch, Wyatt on top of Andy, their lips never once breaking contact. They continued to kiss like touch-starved men, panting and groping and aching for more.

Wyatt's brain had shut off completely. The only thing that mattered was Andy and the perfect warmth of his mouth. Despite being a totally new experience, something about kissing Andy felt like coming home.

When Wyatt rocked his hips forward against him, Andy gasped against his mouth. Wyatt could feel his erection through his jeans pressing against his own. He moved his hips again, grinding his cock against the shape of Andy's, and moaned.

It felt so good. It felt so *right*. Just him and Andy—his best friend—together, kissing and rutting. No camera, no group chat, no tip goals. Just them,

They broke away for a second to catch their breath, and Andy placed his hands on Wyatt's ass, assisting him with his thrusting.

"Fuck, Wyatt, don't stop."

Except, Wyatt did stop.

He froze in place. Hearing his name in Andy's mouth, filled with lust and desire, snapped him back to reality. They weren't filming for FanFrenzy. They weren't doing this for money. They were alone and about to get off with each other for no other reason than their own sexual gratification.

When Wyatt froze, Andy did, too. His eyes went wide, and his cheeks went scarlet. They stared at each other, sharing a look of mild horror and panic.

Then, they jerked away and scrambled gracelessly off the couch, putting as much distance between them as possible.

"I-I had too much to drink," Andy said, wringing his hands.

"Me too," Wyatt said, turning a sickly pale color. "I need to go to bed."

202

"Yeah, me too. Goodnight."

"Goodnight."

They scurried to their respective rooms and slammed the doors shut. Wyatt leaned against the back of his and let out a long, shaky breath. He mentally kicked himself for abandoning his initial instinct—he'd been right from the beginning! Kissing was *far* too intimate.

A wave of nausea swept over him, and he crawled onto his bed, not bothering to get under the covers. The excitement he felt earlier about quitting his job had disappeared and left doubt in its wake. He'd bet everything on FanFrenzy, and now the lines between work and real life blurred and shifted just like the room around him.

He wondered if he'd made a huge mistake.

Chapter Eleven

Things were tense after the kiss. The usual air of casualness and comfort that pervaded their apartment had gone away. Andy and Wyatt exchanged clipped greetings and polite nods while hardly looking at each other.

Regret ate at Andy incessantly. He shouldn't have brought up the conversation of kissing at all, but he wanted to gauge Wyatt's feelings on the subject, to see if they'd changed. *Why* he cared to know Wyatt's feelings, he couldn't say. But he let his curiosity get the better of him, and he was suffering the consequences.

Their live stream on Sunday, two days later, was painfully awkward. It was far more tense and uncomfortable than even their first show had been. There was obvious stiffness in their interactions, no banter between them, and silences stretched far longer than they should've.

The fans picked up on the change right away. Some of them openly speculated in the chat that these two straight boys were losing steam and getting bored with the gay-for-pay lifestyle. Others suggested that the on-screen tension was evidence of one or both of them catching feelings for the other. Andy did his best to laugh off all accusations and lied to cover their asses, telling everyone that they were merely hungover after a night out. Most people bought it, but some weren't convinced. It was honestly a miracle that they'd hit their tip goal at all and that they were both able to get off.

When the show ended, Wyatt excused himself to his room and didn't come out for the rest of the night except when the food delivery guy brought him dinner that evening. He took the bag into his room and ate behind closed doors.

They carried on that way for most of the week, silently avoiding each other and talking only when absolutely necessary. It didn't help that Wyatt was now unemployed and at home 24/7. It made the awkwardness all the more obvious.

Finally, on Thursday morning while pouring his coffee, Wyatt had mumbled the longest string of words to Andy since the kissing incident:

"What's our subscriber count at?"

Andy winced. Since the last show, their numbers weren't heading in the right direction. It had been their first week since starting on this venture together that they'd lost followers. He'd been meaning to talk to him about it but wasn't sure how best to bring it up. It seemed now was as good a time as any.

"We're down a couple hundred," he said.

Wyatt set his mug down too quickly and coffee sloshed onto the countertop. "What? B-But why?"

Andy shrugged apologetically. "There's an optional survey when someone unsubscribes, but not everyone chooses to do it. Of the few that have, some said they just weren't interested in the channel anymore."

But Andy wasn't stupid. He knew the drop in followers had everything to do with how tense their last performance was. It wasn't something he was willing to bring up, though, because it meant talking about what happened after the club.

He so wished that they could just move on and act like it never happened, but Wyatt seemed unable to do that. He still treated Andy more like a stranger than a best friend these days which hurt more than anything.

Wyatt's face paled and he muttered under his breath, "Shit."

Andy knew what he was thinking. Wyatt had just made the leap of faith to quit his job with the belief that FanFrenzy was a safe bet, and now their numbers were dropping. He was going into panic mode. Andy decided to cut off the negative spiral before it took him too far down the rabbit hole.

"I don't think it's going to keep dropping though," Andy said with more confidence than he felt.

Wyatt eyed him warily, "You don't?"

"Nope, because we have a strategy, and we can tweak it if we need to. We'll double down on our efforts and make up for the lost fans. And then some! Promise." He gave him a reassuring smile, and some of the tension left Wyatt's shoulders.

"Maybe you're right," he mumbled, not sounding completely convinced.

"Of course I am," Andy said brightly. "Now, don't stress about it. We'll figure this out. We're in this together, remember?"

"Right…" Wyatt picked up his mug, seemingly lost in thought, and excused himself from the room.

When his bedroom door closed behind him, Andy puffed out a sigh and ran a hand through his hair. Truthfully, he was just as worried as Wyatt was, but one little dip in their subscribers wasn't the end of their porn career by a long shot. They could—no, *would*—recover from this.

He hoped.

———

Later that day at the gym, Andy struggled through his workouts. Normally exercising helped him to get out of his head, but not today. He was too distracted. Thinking about Wyatt and the weirdness between them, thinking about how best to regain the interest of their fans, thinking about what would happen if things fell apart in the end.

His stomach was in knots. He was worried and scared and smoldering with irritation. Things weren't *supposed* to be like this, damnit! It was supposed to be him and Wyatt, having fun, making money, and retiring early. But now, he'd never been more distant from his best friend, and he felt immensely guilty about encouraging him to quit his job in the first place. If FanFrenzy turned out to be a bust, he'd feel like absolute dirt.

An annoyed voice snapped him out of his thoughts.

"Nope! Just *stop*," Leslie ground out.

Andy let the barbell in his hands drop to the ground, huffing in surprise and frustration. "What?"

"What do you mean *what*? Your form is shit and you're going to throw out your damn back!" She folded her arms and stared him down. "What's your problem? You've been off your game all week and now you can't manage a proper deadlift. Spill."

Andy rolled his eyes like a petulant teenager and shuffled over to his water bottle. "It's nothing." He wasn't interested in talking about this with her. It wasn't like she would know how to fix their porn reputation.

"Bullshit. What's eating you?"

"I said it was nothing," he said sourly. In an attempt to put space between them, he made for the stack of fresh towels near the wall.

209

She cut him off, stopping him in his track with a positively lethal glare. Someone as small as she was should not be that intimidating. She pointed an accusing finger in his face, and he flinched as if it were a loaded gun.

"Listen here, you little shit," she snapped. "None of my trainees have ever sustained an injury under my supervision, and I take great pride in that. Proper form is *not* negotiable with me. So, if you're going to disregard everything I've taught you and jerk weights around like a careless asshole, then you can find yourself a new trainer because I'm not interested in watching you hurt yourself."

Andy's face felt hot with embarrassment and guilt. "I-I'm sorry," he said meekly.

She continued to stare him down hard but lowered her finger. "Now tell me what's wrong."

He swallowed. His throat was tight, and he felt suddenly close to tears. It hit him all at once how off-balance everything felt without Wyatt by his side. All of life's stresses were made exponentially more painful by the fact that his best friend was barely talking with him right now.

At that moment, a small squad of elderly ladies walked into the room and made for the treadmills.

"Not here," Andy said, shaking his head.

Leslie nodded and took him to a quiet corner of the gym, near the racquetball courts where hardly anyone went. They sat down on a bench and Andy told her everything— Wyatt quitting his job, the kiss, the awkward live stream, the tension in the apartment, the drop in followers. He didn't hold back any details. Leslie simply sat there quietly, absorbing everything and occasionally asking questions

Once he'd finished, they sat together in silence for a moment while she collected her thoughts.

Finally, after what felt like an eternity, she spoke.

"Well. It sounds like you're in love with him."

Andy gaped at her. "*What?* That's ridiculous! I mean, I love him like a brother, but not like— We're not— I'm not *in* love with him!"

"Dude, it's okay if you are."

"But I'm not gay!"

"So?" she asked with a touch of impatience. "Is he your best friend?"

"Well, yes but that doesn't—"

"And you'd do anything for him?"

"Yeah, but again that doesn't—"

"And you're comfortable having sex with him?"

He hesitated, then cleared his throat. "So far, it's been fine."

"And you *enjoy* having sex with him?"

"It's sex!" he said defensively. "Of course it's enjoyable!"

"But it's not just about your pleasure. You also enjoy making *him* feel good, don't you? That's partly why you practiced giving blowjobs."

Andy's face went warm. "Well, he's my bro..." he mumbled. "I want to make sure it's good for him, too. That doesn't mean I'm in love with him, though."

Leslie gave him an unimpressed look. "Going out on a limb here, but what's the first thing you think about when you wake up?"

Wyatt. Andy blinked, a little surprised by this revelation. When he said nothing, she continued:

"And what's the last thing you think about before going to sleep?"

Again, Wyatt.

He still didn't say anything. Just shrugged noncommittally. She wasn't buying it though. She narrowed her shrewd eyes at him.

"And what if I told you that he stopped by the gym recently to sign up for a membership and ended up asking me to go on a date with him? We're meeting for dinner this Friday."

Andy's mind went blank of everything except bitter jealousy and outrage.

"What?!" he snapped. "But— He said we were exclusive! We shook on it! And *you* have a boyfriend! I can't believe you'd do that!"

Had he been using his rational brain, he would've realized that this scenario was ridiculous for many reasons. The odds of Wyatt meeting and asking out Leslie were slim to none. When would he have had time to sign up for a membership anyway? His routine for the past year consisted only of going to work and coming straight home. And how would Leslie even recognize him? They'd never met. Anyone could've seen how absurd it all was. But the trouble was that Andy *wasn't* using his rational brain.

Leslie gave him a satisfied smirk. "Chill out. I was kidding."

He opened his mouth, ready to spit venom, and then closed it. "You— He didn't ask you out?"

"Nope." She cocked her head at him curiously, "Do you normally get that jealous when your friends have dinner dates?"

Andy's lips thinned and he folded his arms. "He and I made an agreement together. I'd be upset if he broke it. That's all."

"Right," she said dryly. "And you're positive it couldn't be something more than that?"

The idea of him having feelings for Wyatt was ludicrous, and he wasn't interested in humoring her. He stuck his chin out proudly and looked the other way.

She sighed, and he could practically hear her accompanying eyeroll. But when she finally spoke, her voice was soft.

"It's okay if you love him as more than a friend, but just be careful. Mixing transactional sex with genuine feelings is a messy combo. Someone's bound to get hurt. Maybe it's time to put an end to this cam modeling thing. I know you don't want to let him down, but maybe it's best for your friendship in the long run." She rose from the bench. "I think we should wrap it up early today. Get some rest and try to come back with a clear head. No more half-assed form, okay?"

Andy mumbled a vague affirmative but let her go. He sat there for ages thinking about what she'd said. *Did* he love Wyatt? The idea should've been laughable, and yet he was having a hard time finding the humor in it.

Yes, he did care deeply for him, but he was his best friend—of course he cared. However, they were also having sex and Andy couldn't pretend that he didn't like it. Sucking Wyatt's cock should've felt like a chore but, on the contrary, it turned him on. And unlike butt stuff, enjoying the act sucking dick couldn't be easily explained away with a prostate. The pleasure he got from deepthroating was, in part, psychological. It was the knowledge that his best friend was the one stretching his lips wide. It was hearing him moan and feeling his thighs shake as he neared orgasm. It was feeling his release pump down his throat. It was knowing he was making Wyatt feel good.

On top of that, Andy had enjoyed kissing him. *Really* enjoyed it. Since the incident, he dreamed about kissing him again every night this week, feeling their tongues reunite, relishing the warmth of his mouth…

No—the idea of him loving Wyatt wasn't laughable at all. Because he realized deep down, buried beneath miles of denial and shame, he did love him.

Shit.

Chapter Twelve

Wyatt lay in his bed and stared at the ceiling mulling over his predicament. He no longer had a stable 9-to-5 job and their follower count was going in the wrong direction. Anxiety writhed in his stomach as he thought about the potential of losing everything. He had a decent amount in savings thanks to the FanFrenzy work they'd done up to that point, but that would only get him so far. And after seeing Andy struggle for months to find work, he worried that he might suffer the same fate, desperately scrambling to find another job only to end up in retail earning minimum wage.

No. He wouldn't let that happen.

Andy was right—they were in this together. They'd figure out a way to fix this before things fell apart. Maybe it was time to amp things up a bit with their next show; do something that was sure to generate some buzz.

Except...

He closed his eyes and sighed. Except that things had been weird between him and Andy ever since that night they went to the club. Wyatt acknowledged that he wasn't doing anything to alleviate the tension in the house, but he was still freaking out about the kiss. As much as he wanted to blame the alcohol, he'd been much too sober at that time to claim he wasn't acting in his right mind. He knew what he was doing, and he knew what he was feeling. While it may have started out as an innocent suggestion to practice kissing, desire and arousal quickly became his primary motivation. He *wanted* Andy.

It was still a hard truth to swallow. He didn't understand *why* he wanted him—he was straight. And yet his mouth ached to know his; he yearned to feel his body beneath him.

He felt like a fucking creep.

Andy was his best friend, and he deserved better than that. Sure, Andy seemed to be enjoying himself while they kissed, but Andy was someone who could separate sex from feelings. Wyatt apparently wasn't. If Andy realized that Wyatt had feelings for him, he'd be disgusted.

"I don't have feelings for him," he muttered to himself miserably, trying to believe the words he was saying. But his voice lacked conviction.

He scrubbed a hand over his face and tried to rationalize the situation. Maybe there was some way that he didn't like Andy romantically after all. He considered the facts:

Fact #1: Andy was his bro. His *best* bro.

Fact #2: He felt more comfortable around Andy than anybody else (see Fact #1).

Fact #3: He and Andy had been having sex together for several weeks now for the sake of money.

Fact #4: Feelings are super complicated and often unreliable. So, it was possible that the natural affection he felt for Andy as a friend got tangled up with all the dopamine from sex and led him to *believe* that he liked him romantically.

Wyatt blinked. Of course! He didn't *really* like Andy in that way. This whole thing was just some weird chemical mix-up in his brain. That's all. And so long as he understood that, there was nothing to worry about. Those feelings for

Andy were just an illusion, and he knew better than to feed into them.

Some of the tension that he'd been holding in his body for the past week melted away. This revelation came as a huge relief because he missed Andy terribly. Not talking with him or hanging out had been miserable, but now he could put that silly kiss behind them and go back to the way things used to be. Also, he felt more optimistic about their next FanFrenzy show. He and Andy *were* a team, and they *would* figure out how to make up for their losses.

The front door opened and shut. Andy was back from the gym. Feeling a surge of determination and excitement, Wyatt rolled out of bed and emerged from his room.

"Hey, you're back," Wyatt smiled.

Andy paused in the kitchen, watching him warily. His body was stiff with uncertainty. "Uh. Hey, man. What's up?"

"I thought about what you said before, and you were right. Our follower count will bounce back. In fact, I had an idea for our next show."

Andy cocked an eyebrow. He still seemed unsure about Wyatt's sudden change in behavior. "Really?"

"Yeah, but we don't have to talk about work right this second. I've been itching to play a round of *Street Kombat 7*. You down?"

Relief appeared to wash over the muscles in Andy's body, and his face brightened. But Wyatt noted that there was something else there, too. Something at odds with the happiness in his eyes. Despite it, he gave him a wide grin and said, "You're on. Loser orders pizza."

Wyatt laughed. "Deal."

———

Kneeling between Andy's thighs, Wyatt started having second thoughts about his plan. He didn't think he'd have any hangups, but as he slicked lube along the length of Andy's dildo with his palm, he became suddenly aware of how obscene this was.

Andy adjusted the pillow beneath his head and then took the bottle of lube from him, pouring some onto his fingers and massaging it onto his pink hole. Wyatt stared in wonderment as he slipped one and then two fingers inside himself. He swallowed thickly and felt his face and neck redden. Seeing Andy like this—laid out on the bed, legs in the air, vulnerable—felt like encroaching on his privacy. Of course, he knew it wasn't. He had permission to be there, to watch.

Slipping in a third finger, Andy's head lulled back, and he let out a small, frustrated noise. Wyatt couldn't tell if this was enjoyable for him or not.

"Does it feel good?" he asked shyly.

Brows furrowed in concentration, Andy nodded. "It feels amazing. It's just awkward trying to reach the prostate from this angle."

"Oh." Wyatt watched with curiosity as Andy's fingers worked in and out. "So, um, where is it?"

"The prostate? Well, from where you're sitting, you'd want to go in a few inches and hook your fingers upward, like this." He demonstrated with his free hand. "You'll know when you've found it."

"Why? Does it feel weird or something?"

He laughed, "No, not particularly. You'll know because it feels fucking amazing. When I first found mine, I almost came immediately."

"Oh," Wyatt said again. "Well, what if I was looking for someone else's, not my own? How would I know when I found it?"

222

Andy raised an eyebrow at him, a question in his eyes. They'd only discussed using a dildo for today's show. Wyatt had been too squeamish at the idea of putting his fingers inside him.

"Well, in that case," he continued, "your partner would probably let you know." He gave him a wry grin. "Trust me, it's not that hard to find."

Suddenly, there was a chime from the computer notifying them that someone had donated. They both looked at the screen. It seemed that people in the group chat were enjoying their conversation. They'd also been excited about today's tip goals just as Wyatt had hoped they would be. They reached their goals much faster than they had during last week's show.

Wyatt cleared his throat and looked back at Andy, giving the dildo a little wave. "Ready?"

Andy glanced back at the screen once more to ensure that they were centered in the frame and then nodded. "Let's do this."

Wyatt lined up the tip of the dildo with Andy's puckered entrance and slowly pressed it in. As the head made it past his tight ring of muscle, Andy let out a soft groan and pushed his hips back to encourage Wyatt to go deeper. When it was fully in, Wyatt's fingers, which were gripping the set of fake balls, were pressed against the heat of Andy's hole. His throat worked.

"Okay," Andy mumbled after a moment. "Start fucking me."

Those words sent a shiver down Wyatt's spine straight to his hard cock. It twitched between his legs and a glistening bead of precum leaked out of his slit. Without a word, he pulled the dildo out slowly before pressing it back in again to the hilt. Andy's eyes fluttered closed and his mouth fell open.

"Oh, fuck," he breathed. "That's so good. Just like that."

Wyatt continued, setting a steady pace, and watching as Andy's cock occasionally jumped and twitched. It must've been his prostate. With every involuntary movement of his dick, his pink hole squeezed around the long, life-like dick. Wyatt's mouth watered at the sight, and he wondered what it would feel like to have Andy's muscles tighten around him.

"Don't stop," Andy whined, spreading his cheeks with his hands in an attempt to take the dildo deeper.

Wyatt's cock was painfully hard now, and a thick stream of precum dripped down his shaft. It was as if his body was self-lubricating, readying to fuck.

Andy's lidded, half-glazed eyes met his. When he spoke, his voice was rough and filled with need. "More. *Please.*"

Without thinking, Wyatt pulled out the dildo completed, slid two of his own fingers into Andy's warmth, and hooked them upwards just like he'd been shown. He apparently found was he was looking for because Andy gasped in surprise as he pressed the pads of his thick fingers against the small bundle of nerves inside him.

"Holy shit," he panted. "Keep doing that."

Neither of them seemed to care that they'd gone off script. They were both thoroughly lost in the moment.

Wyatt continued to massage that sweet spot in Andy and watched him writhe helplessly on his fingers, begging for more. He slipped a third finger in, earning him a needy moan. The sensation of Andy's hole pulsing and flexing around him made Wyatt dizzy with lust. His cock ached to be in his fingers' place.

Even in the haze of his arousal, the realization struck him with frightening clarity: *He wanted to fuck Andy.* And

225

not just with a dildo. He wanted to bury his cock in his ass until it couldn't go any farther and fuck him silly before pumping his cum deep inside him. He wanted to make Andy feel good, to feel their bodies unite, to make him cry out in pleasure, to give him the best orgasm of his life.

The immense hunger he felt for Andy's body shook him to his core, and he tried in vain to remind himself that this was all just some weird chemical mix-up in his head. But his desire was overwhelming, and the only thing he could think about at that moment was satisfying Andy.

He wrapped his free hand around Andy's cock and began stroking while finger-fucking him. Loud moans rose from the back of Andy's throat and filled the room. His body had become blotchy and flushed with pleasure, he fisted the blankets beneath him, and he looked at Wyatt with a pleading, stormy look in his eyes.

Wyatt leaned over him, and Andy instinctively sat up on his elbows, allowing their lips to meet halfway. Their mouths met eagerly, crashing together and seeking out each other's tongues. Andy's breath hitched and one arm wrapped around Wyatt's neck.

Wyatt jerked him faster and applied more pressure to his prostate. Moments later, Andy cried out and his body tensed as his orgasm erupted between then, painting his chest and abs. Wyatt's painfully stiff cock wept with need as Andy's hole squeezed tightly around his fingers. He grabbed his dick and after only a few strokes, he came so hard he saw stars. The only thing keeping him grounded was the steady presence of Andy's lips pressed against his.

Once they caught their breath, Andy slumped back against the bed, thoroughly spent, and whimpered as Wyatt withdrew his fingers. They stared at each other as a beat of uncertainty passed between them.

Finally, Andy gave him a cheeky smile and said, "I told you that you wouldn't have any trouble finding the prostate."

Wyatt laughed out loud. "It was probably just beginner's luck."

"Or natural talent," Andy offered.

He smiled a bashful smile and looked away. It was hard to imagine that he had any kind of natural talent for gay sex. Perhaps what Andy had really meant was that he had a natural talent for pleasuring him specifically. His ears burned at the thought.

It was then that they both noticed the perpetual chiming noise from the computer. There was a steady stream of tips coming in from fans. The group chat was going wild.

They were back in the game.

Chapter Thirteen

That night after the show, Andy was scrolling through their FanFrenzy profile, watching in awe as followers continued to pour in. Since the broadcast, they'd gotten a massive influx of new subscribers. Eleven thousand and counting.

At the moment they were at twenty-seven thousand followers total, which meant that they would be pulling in $2.5 million a year (if they could maintain their viewership, of course). The numbers were utterly dizzying, and he and Wyatt celebrated with a nice dinner out at a fancy restaurant they never would've splurged on with their old jobs. Andy noted that they both avoided touching any kind of alcohol—obviously the incident after the club was still fresh in their minds. Not that it really made any difference. He and Wyatt were on good terms again, and apparently kissing was now a part of their show. It was a relief to taste Wyatt's mouth again, to feel the heat of his mouth. Andy ached for it ever since that first night, and he felt like a bit of an addict. He'd only just kissed him earlier that day and already he missed his lips. If Wyatt ever found out how much he ached for his touch, he'd be appalled.

A direct message came in, pulling Andy from his thoughts. He clicked on it and saw that a fan had sent him a link to an off-site page. Their accompanying message said:

Did you guys know this was a thing?! LOL

Normally, Andy wouldn't click on strange links sent by strange people, but he vaguely recognized the name of the website—FrenzyFiction. So, he followed the link and discovered that it was a site dedicated to fan fiction about FanFrenzy models. What's more, there were approximately fourteen different stories written about him and Wyatt of varying length and content ratings. He was in disbelief. People actually cared enough to write stories about them? The whole thing was a little surreal. But he'd be lying if he said he wasn't at least a little curious. So, he clicked on the story at the top of the page, the one that had been "fingered" the most (on FrenzyFiction, the "like" system had been replaced with the "finger" system... Charming).

Andy spent the next hour reading a fifteen-thousand-word story, spanning six chapters, in which he and Wyatt slowly fell in love with each other between their FanFrenzy broadcasts. It was...surprisingly well-written. Of course, the writer had gotten a lot of things wrong about their apartment layout and personal lives, but the dialog between them was shockingly on-brand. He could practically hear Wyatt's voice throughout the story which was simultaneously creepy and oddly compelling.

By the time he finished, Andy was on the verge of tears—which frustrated him because he *wasn't* a cryer. But he could hardly contain the emotions bubbling up inside him. Reading about him and Wyatt declaring their love for each other yanked painfully on his heartstrings because he knew he could never have that. Since his conversation with Leslie, he'd still been in denial about the true depth of his feelings for Wyatt, but now, after seeing some fictional version of himself get the thing he so desperately wanted, he couldn't deny any longer that he was, in fact, desperately and hopelessly in love with his best friend. It was a devastating realization.

He couldn't go on like this.

With every broadcast they did together, Andy realized that he was falling harder and harder for Wyatt. There was no way he could keep this up for a couple of years like they'd initially planned. If he didn't break things off soon, the damage would be irreparable. Their friendship could fall apart completely, and that possibility was unthinkable to Andy. No amount of money was worth that risk. What was the point of early retirement if he couldn't spend it with his best friend?

On top of everything else, he felt a pang of deep, searing guilt as Leslie's words from their conversation months ago rang in his head: *No more secrets!* He was being dishonest with Wyatt. They'd agreed to embark on this business venture together as friends, but since Andy's feelings had grown into something more, there was no longer a mutual understanding and agreement between them. Every touch Wyatt placed onto his body only fed the fires of Andy's desire, and Wyatt was none the wiser. It wasn't fair to him. Secretly enjoying and savoring Wyatt's touch as a lover was wrong on so many levels.

The lies had to stop. While Andy wasn't prepared to confess his love for Wyatt, he could at least end things before it got worse. And maybe, by ending everything now, he stood a chance to move on from his feelings, and they could return to just being friends...

He knew what he had to do.

————

The following morning, Andy stepped out of his bedroom wearing his gym clothes. Wyatt was sitting on the couch eating a bowl of cereal and watching TV.

Upon seeing Andy, he grinned, "I don't think I'm ever going to get tired of sleeping in." He took notice of Andy's clothes and cocked his head. "Going to the gym early today?"

Andy nodded. "Yeah. I'm in the mood for a run. But I was wondering if I could talk with you first.

Sensing the serious tone, Wyatt grabbed the remote and turned off the television. "What's up?"

Andy hesitated for a second, looking at the empty spot on the couch beside Wyatt, but ultimately decided it was better to stand, to give them some space. He took a breath and stared down at the carpet, working up the nerve to say what he knew he had to say.

Finally, he spoke. "I think our next broadcast should be our last."

Wyatt's eyes went wide with shock and confusion. He set down his cereal on the coffee table. "What? *Why?*"

He still avoided his gaze. "I think we've been pushing our luck."

Wyatt furrowed his brows. "What are you talking about? Our profile's popularity is exploding. People love us!"

"We're in over our heads, Wyatt."

"Don't tell me you're getting cold feet now. Getting a ton of followers was all part of the plan! What about retiring early?"

Andy let out a frustrated sigh and scrubbed a hand over his face. "Look, I don't think this is good for our friendship, okay?"

Wyatt fell silent. "...Our friendship? What do you mean?"

"I mean that friends don't have sex with each other!"

"But you said—"

"I know what I said!" he said louder than he intended to. Wyatt gave him a hurt look, and Andy winced, sighing again. "I'm sorry, I didn't mean to yell. It's just— I know this is all my fault. I talked you into this thing. I was the one who kept saying that this was only a job and that the sex part didn't have to be a big deal. But it's hard for things to feel like old times after everything we've done together."

A heavy silence passed between them.

Wyatt asked quietly, "Where is this all coming from?"

"I just—" Andy squeezed his eyes shut and shook his head. "I just want to go back to the way things used to be between us."

"Andy, I quit my job for this…"

"I-I know. I'm sorry I dragged you into it. And I'm sorry I'm letting you down. But there's enough in savings for you to take the next two years off to find work if you needed to. And if nothing else, this was a good motivator to finally cut ties with Sue Ellen. So, it wasn't all for nothing, right?"

Wyatt said nothing. He just set his jaw and turned to look out the window, his frustration rolling off of him in waves. Seeing him so upset pained Andy but he knew he was still making the right decision. They would eventually move past this. One day, they would be able to look back on everything and laugh about how crazy and ridiculous they'd been. The details of what they did with each other's bodies would grow hazy and vague with time, and the entire affair would be reduced to just another amusing anecdote about their wild years. And most importantly of all, they would still be friends.

This was for the best.

Andy swallowed around the lump in his throat and said, "I don't want to do this anymore. I'm sorry."

Then he left the apartment, closing the door behind him without sparing Wyatt another glance.

Chapter Fourteen

Wyatt's bowl of cereal grew soggy and warm on the coffee table. He'd lost his appetite. That morning he had woken up feeling good. The show yesterday had been amazing, the fancy dinner they'd shared together was delicious, and the follower count continued to rise. He'd been able to make peace with the fact that he wanted to fuck Andy because he kept reminding himself that the mixed signals his brain was sending to his body were to blame—it had nothing to do with having feelings for Andy.

But now, in the aftermath of the bomb Andy had dropped, his good mood was in shambles. He felt anger and confusion and hopelessness and…something else. It felt suspiciously like loss. As if some part of him was grieving the end of their broadcasts, the end of being naked together, touching and kissing and getting off. The idea that he would miss spending that time with Andy was absurd. Why would he miss having sex with a dude?

Well... Maybe it wasn't *that* absurd. After all, doing that stuff with Andy was novel and fun. Also, it felt good. Like, *really* good. Okay—there was a small possibility that it had been the best sex of his life, but he was reluctant to admit that. He probably only felt that way because he hadn't gotten laid in ages before he started FanFrenzy.

Still, he couldn't deny that he was disappointed this was all ending. Part of it was the money. They were making an insane amount now and were totally on track to realize their dreams of retiring before thirty. But there was another part of him that was disappointed that he'd never get the chance to fuck Andy. They'd come this far in their sexual exploration, and Andy clearly liked things in his ass. It was honestly a shame they wouldn't be able to try it at least once. (He could hardly believe he was thinking this way; a few weeks ago, the idea of fucking Andy was completely out of the question.)

Andy's voice rang through his head then. *I don't think this is good for our friendship...*

Those words sat on his shoulders like something heavy and dangerous. He was reminded of going to New Orleans in high school with his parents. A street performer in the French Quarter with a huge yellow Burmese python was letting people take pictures with it on their shoulders and Wyatt had gotten his taken. Andy's words felt like that—something seemingly innocuous that had the power to wrap itself around his body and squeeze the life from him at any moment.

His thoughts began to wander. Maybe his desire to fuck Andy wasn't just about physical gratification. Maybe there was something deeper making him ache for his body. Had Andy sensed that? Is that what he meant by *this isn't good for our friendship*? What if Andy had seen something in him that he couldn't see in himself? What if everything he was feeling wasn't just a chemical mix-up in his brain?

The python was wrapping itself around his neck and starting to squeeze...

Wyatt jumped off the couch, chest heaving, and stormed to his bedroom. He would *not* let himself follow that train of thought. He had things to do and plans to make. Andy was right that they had enough earnings from FanFrenzy to float for a while, but pissing away all of his savings didn't make sense to Wyatt's financially-minded brain. He needed to find a new job.

He grabbed his laptop and clicked around through several job listing sites. All of the listings for Payroll Specialists seemed just as bleak and uninspiring as his last role. Some of them paid better than his old job, but none of them were anywhere close to what they were making with FanFrenzy. That was to be expected though. And of course they sounded boring—he was looking at job listings, not amusement parks. But boring was fine. So long as he didn't end up with another Sue Ellen for a manager, he could do it. He could totally spend the next thirty years of his life at a desk in a drab little office processing payroll before finally retiring when the best years of his life were behind him. Easy peasy...

A notification popped up letting him know he had a new email. He opened it and saw that it was from the HR manager of his old job. It said that after a "thorough investigation" they determined that the recent mass exodus from the Payroll Department was due to "gross abuse of managerial power." As such, they decided to dismiss the previous manager (ie. Sue Ellen) and hire a replacement who was a "better fit" for the company's culture. The email ended with them offering him his job back with a $5000 increase to his salary. It seemed that they were desperate to fill in vacancies after half the team walked out.

Wyatt stared at the email for a long time, mulling over the offer. Without Sue Ellen, the job would be way more tolerable (assuming her replacement was a semi-decent human being). And the pay increase was nice. But still, returning to the same boring job he'd been doing for the past year was hardly an exciting prospect. Also, HR had known about Sue Ellen's shitty behavior for *years* and did fuck all about it. Apparently, it took her literally throwing a fax machine across the office for them to acknowledge her hostility. He had very little confidence that the HR team would be helpful if he needed them in the future.

Then again, he had very little confidence that he would find any job that was half as exciting as getting paid to have sex with his favorite person.

Fuck, he didn't want this to be over.

———

When Andy finally came back home from the gym, Wyatt was waiting for him on one of the bartop stools. Andy stopped in his tracks, watching him warily.

"If you want to stop doing FanFrenzy, that's okay," Wyatt said calmly. "But I think we should leave our account active for at least the next six months even if we're not making new content. I know we're going to lose most of our followers, but there might still be newcomers who discover us later and want to watch our old stuff. It might be a good way to make passive incoming for a while."

Andy set his water bottle down on the counter and nodded slowly, "That sounds okay to me."

"Also," Wyatt continued, "I think we should bring out the big guns for our last show. Go out with a bang and generate as much buzz and money as possible."

His eyes went wide. "You don't mean…"

Wyatt nodded. Then added, "We don't have to if you don't want to."

Andy chewed on his lip, obviously thinking it over. The expression on his face was equal parts doubtful and eager. Despite keeping a steady poker face, Wyatt was feeling the same way. He both wanted the opportunity to fuck Andy but also feared what it might do to him emotionally. There was a chance he simply needed to get this out of his system. However, there was also the chance that it might just confuse him further. There was only one way to find out.

Finally, Andy squared his shoulders and looked decided. "Let's do it."

Wyatt's heart pounded excitedly in his chest, but his face still did not betray his emotions. "Are you sure?"

"Yes. Like you said, it's our final show— We should go out with a bang."

They shook on it.

Chapter Fifteen

Andy had decided not to make an announcement about their next show being their final one. It would be better to break the news via a text post afterward. He didn't want to deal with all of the questions in the group chat about their decision. He simply wanted to focus on what he and Wyatt were about to do. His body hungered for Wyatt's, and while getting fucked might ultimately deepen his romantic feelings, that was a risk he was willing to take. It was reckless, but he also knew he'd never get another opportunity to like this ever again. And if Wyatt was okay with it, then he saw no reason why he shouldn't enjoy this last hoorah.

"Hey everyone," Andy smiled, waving at the camera. "We've got a special show for y'all today. Jack and I are going to do something we never imagined we would do together. We've gotten so many requests for this, though, we had a change of heart." That wasn't a total lie; Andy got DMs daily asking if they were ever going to fuck. "If we hit our tip goal today, I'll let Jack fuck me."

The group chat exploded.

OMGGG IT'S HAPPENING!! IT'S HAPPENING!!!!!

asdfghjklgdfghjkl

HOLY SHIT.

oh my god i'm freaking the fuck OUT!!

FINALLY!!!

At long last!

I never believed in miracles but now I do LOL :P

Despite his nerves, Andy laughed at the reaction. He looked over at Wyatt who was quieter than usual today. He smiled at the messages pouring in but didn't say anything. There was something off about him. Andy wondered if he was having second thoughts about this. He'd asked him this morning before the show if he was still sure he wanted to do this, and he said yes. Andy wasn't sure what to make of his behavior but decided it wasn't the time to dwell.

He turned back to the chat and said, "Like I said, I'll Jack fuck me *if* we hit our tip goal! It's a bit higher than normal because if I'm taking a dick up my ass then it had better be worth it." Of course, he would take Wyatt's dick for free, but they didn't need to know that.

When he launched their tip goal of $5000, donations came flooding in immediately. The largest contribution—three grand—was made by their old friend str8boyaddict.

"Thank you, str8boy," Andy grinned. For a moment, he reflected on the fact that none of this would be happening had it not been for str8boy's initial dare to fuck himself in Wyatt's bed. How different things would be right now if he hadn't gotten caught. Wyatt would still probably be at his old job, and Andy would still be secretly filming porn and dancing around the truth. In some ways, things were better than they were. In other ways, they were worse.

In less than a minute, they reached their tip goals and donations were *still* coming in. People were clearly excited. By the time the dust settled, they'd made a little more than $8000 in tips alone.

Andy looked at Wyatt and gave him a lopsided smile. "The people have spoken. You ready?"

Wyatt returned the smile and nodded. "Let's do it."

They pulled Andy's desk closer to the bed so that the laptop camera could capture everything more clearly; then they climbed onto the mattress, kneeling in front of each other, and paused for a moment, just staring into the other's eyes. Andy lost himself in Wyatt's familiar blues, and silence seemed to settle around them. Suddenly, they were the only two people in the world. Everything else faded into the background.

Wyatt's stare was intense, focused, and smoldering with want. It sent a shiver down Andy's spine. He wanted nothing more than to tear his clothes off and jump on his cock that instant, but he was also acutely aware that this was the last time he'd have permission to look at Wyatt like this, to touch his body, to press his lips against his. He wanted to savor every moment.

He leaned forward and placed a small, gentle kiss on the corner of his mouth. Wyatt's eyes fluttered closed, and he took a steadying breath. Andy placed another kiss on him, this time on the cheek. Next, on his brow, on his temple, on the bridge of his nose. He wanted to kiss every inch of him, but he knew there wasn't time; his brain quietly reminded him that people were watching and waiting.

Finally, he cupped Wyatt's face in his hands and drew their lips together. Their connection was shy and sweet at first, but their mouths gradually became needier, more insistent. Soon, they were panting and groping and tugging at the other's clothes. Andy sucked on Wyatt's tongue as one of his sturdy hands pawed him through his jeans. A small whine escaped the back of Andy's throat, and he felt a satisfied smile spread on Wyatt's lips.

They parted only for a moment to pull off their shirts and shimmy out of their shorts, tossing them away haphazardly. When their mouths reconvened, there was a greater sense of urgency between them. Wyatt wrapped his strong arms around Andy's waist and pulled their bodies flush together. Andy moaned as he felt Wyatt's hot, throbbing cock press against his abs. His own dick was painfully hard and rubbing against Wyatt's stomach, leaving a trail of precum on his skin. He raked his fingers down Wyatt's shoulders and back, appreciating the firm muscles and trying to pull him closer still. They were as close as they could possibly be, but it wasn't enough. He wanted their physical boundaries to dissolve entirely, for their bodies to melt together and become one. He wanted Wyatt inside of him, filling him, completing him.

The reasonable part of himself that wanted to savor the moment was being drowned out by the raw animal need to be fucked *immediately*. He pulled his mouth away from Wyatt's, breathing heavily, and leaned in close to his ear. He spoke low, keeping his secret between them.

"I need you inside me."

Wyatt's breath hitched for a second before crashing his mouth against Andy's again and gently guiding him down to the bed. Laying on top of him now, he trailed kisses along his jaw and neck and collarbone, down across his chest and along his abs, before reaching his erection. He placed several kisses along the underside of Andy's cock, causing him to gasp. Then, he hooked his hands under Andy's knees and lifted, spreading his legs into the air and exposing his eager pink hole.

Before Andy could process what was about to happen, Wyatt plunged his mouth down. He let out a small groan of surprise and pleasure as Wyatt began sucking on the sensitive strip of flesh between his ass and balls. The wetness of his mouth and lips drove Andy wild, and he writhed under his touch, bucking his hips. Then, Wyatt's hot tongue traveled downward, and he licked and probed and lapped at his puckered entrance. Andy let out another gasp. *Holy fuck.*

He buried his fists in Wyatt's hair and stared down at him in amazement. Wyatt's eyes met his, but he never stopped using his mouth. The sight was simultaneously the hottest and most obscene thing he'd ever seen. His best friend was eating him out and making eye contact while he did it. There was a possessive and hungry look in his eyes.

Wyatt pushed his tongue inside and Andy's grip on his hair instinctively tightened.

"Oh, fuck," he groaned, fighting the urge to let his head roll back against the pillow. He didn't want to look away. He wanted to remember this moment as clearly as possible.

With a pleased look on his face, Wyatt spread Andy's cheeks further apart and began tongue-fucking him. Andy tugged gently on his hair, pulling him deeper inside. Wyatt moaned and it rumbled through Andy's body, vibrating his prostate. *Sweet baby Jesus.* He couldn't wait any longer. His prostate begged for contact, and as hot as getting eaten out was, only Wyatt's cock could satiate him.

"Need more," he whined deliriously. "Need you."

Wyatt seemed to understand what he meant because he sat back on his heels and wrapped his lips around one of his fingers, before drawing it out of his mouth and pressing it into Andy. A second later, he slipped in a second and scissored them inside him. Andy panted and rocked his hips, desperate for more.

"I'm ready," he said breathlessly. Wyatt had barely prepped him at all, but that didn't matter. His body was ready for him.

"Are you sure?" Wyatt asked with a hint of doubt in his voice.

Andy nodded. "Yes, I am. *Please.*"

Wyatt didn't ask again. He opened the bottle of lube and coated his cock generously. Then, with slicked-up fingers, he massaged the excess onto Andy's hole. It pulsed eagerly in response as if anticipating what was coming next. He shifted forward, aligning himself, and then slowly pushed in.

All coherent thought left Andy's head as Wyatt's thick, heavy cock slid inside him, grinding against his sweet spot every inch of the way. Finally, he bottomed out, and Andy felt Wyatt's hips run up against his ass.

Wyatt leaned forward and pressed a kiss to his lips. "Holy fuck, you're so tight. No one's ever taken all of me before."

Hearing his voice brought Andy's mind back to reality, and it struck him then with dizzying clarity—*Wyatt was inside of him.* His best friend's cock was buried in his ass to the hilt. He'd wanted this for so long, and finally, his wish had been granted. It was better than he could've imagined. Fuck, he felt so *full.* Wyatt was significantly thicker than his dildo, and his girth stretched him like he'd never been stretched before. It felt *right.* Like they were completing each other somehow.

Andy kissed him back and said softly, "You feel amazing."

Wyatt's cheeks flushed bashfully, and he kissed him again, slow and deep. He started moving his hips, rocking them in and out, dragging out low breathy noises from Andy. With every thrust inward, Andy felt Wyatt's balls slap against him.

Wyatt kneeled back and grabbed Andy's waist, pulling him back to meet his bucking hips. He set a delicious, steady rhythm, and the titillating sound of skin slapping against skin filled the air. His eyes roamed over Andy's body hungrily before reaching out a hand and rubbing it across his abs and chest. That caressing touch spoke volumes. *You look incredible*, it said. Andy had never felt so sexy in his entire life as he did at that moment, watching Wyatt indulge the obvious desire to touch his body.

Andy soaked in the sight of Wyatt. Broad chest, sculpted pecs, strong arms. The deep blush spreading across his face and neck brought out the beautiful color in his eyes. How had he never noticed in their college years how gorgeous he was? Everything about his was perfect.

Wyatt's pace became faster and stronger, all the while watching Andy carefully as if to ensure that it was still good for him, too. That care and concern melted Andy from the inside, and his love for him grew. Some distant part of his brain was screaming at him about how much harder he was making things for himself, how it would be impossible to get over him at this rate. But Andy paid the voice no mind. His senses were too absorbed in the perfection of Wyatt—the sight of him, the sounds rumbling lowly in his throat, the soothing scent of his body wash and sweat, the warmth of his hands, and the thickness of his cock. He was in heaven.

Andy grabbed Wyatt's firm ass and encouraged him deeper inside. Wyatt obliged and began drilling into him with every bit of power he possessed. A long, love-drunk moan floated out of Andy unknowingly. From the base of his loins, he felt a tremendous pressure building rapidly. He wasn't even touching his own cock, but at this rate, he didn't need to. He was going to come.

He managed to breathe out a hitched word of warning. "*I'm—*"

Understanding what Andy was trying to say, Wyatt licked his lips and doubled down on his thrusts. He was fucking him so hard that stars were beginning to swim in Andy's vision.

"*Don't stop!*" he gasped, gripping Wyatt's muscles for dear life.

Wyatt's thighs trembled violently as his movements became erratic and choppy. A few more thrusts against his prostate pushed Andy over the edge and, without touching his cock at all, he cried out as he spilled hot release against his belly. It wasn't like a normal orgasm; it seemed to pour out of him in a thick, steady stream. His brain stopped completely, and the world ceased to exist for a moment. It was like he'd undergone a factory reset.

As his orgasm rippled through his body, his hole tightened and squeezed against Wyatt's cock, and that was all it took for him to lose himself, too. He grunted and bucked wildly, unloading rope after rope of cum into Andy until his balls were completely emptied. Eventually, his cock stopped twitching and jerking, and he collapsed down onto him, trying to catch his breath.

When Andy's thoughts finally came back online, he felt only immense satisfaction and contentment. And love. He carded his fingers tenderly through Wyatt's hair and hummed happily, basking in the afterglow.

"I love you," he said drowsily.

Wyatt went rigid on top of him, and Andy froze as he realized what he'd just said. Icy fear ran through his veins.

Oh my God. Fuck, fuck, fuck.

Wyatt pulled back and looked at him, surprise and confusion plastered on his face. Andy probably should've tried talking his way out of it somehow, coming up with some excuse or saying that he meant it as a friend. But he had no words. All he could do was stare back at him in stunned, terrified silence.

After a beat, Wyatt reached for the laptop and closed it, ending the broadcast and shutting down the group chat. Andy thought the worst—he must've been pissed and didn't want witnesses for the conversation they were about to have.

But when Wyatt faced him again, his expression was unreadable. "Do you mean that? Do you really love me?"

Andy's mind screamed at him: *Deny it! Deny it!* But then he remembered Leslie's words again. *No more secrets.* Maybe it would've been wiser to lie for the sake of preserving their friendship, but he couldn't bring himself to do it. As scared as he was, he didn't want to lie to Wyatt anymore. He loved him too much for that.

So, he swallowed around the lump in his throat and nodded.

Wyatt studied him for a moment longer and Andy squirmed under his gaze. It was then that he realized that Wyatt was still inside of him, and he'd hardly softened at all. That was weird… If Wyatt was angry about this, you'd think that he would've—

Wyatt pressed his lips to Andy's, and Andy gasped in surprise, before melting into his warmth. When Wyatt pulled away again, Andy looked at him with furrowed brows, his eyes full of questions and hope.

Wyatt smiled softly. "I love you, too, Andrew."

Andy blinked. Had he blacked out from the sex? Was this all a dream? He couldn't believe it.

"Come again?"

Wyatt laughed. "I said, I love you, too. As in, I'm *in* love with you."

A small smile tugged at Andy's mouth, and it stretched into a wide, dazzlingly grin. He crashed his mouth into Wyatt's and wrapped his arms around his neck. He could feel Wyatt's smile against his own. Andy wasn't sure how long they kissed—it could've been minutes or hours—but when they finally pulled away, they were panting lightly and Wyatt rested his forehead against Andy's. He moved his hips slowly, sliding his cock in and out of his spent hole. It wasn't even about sex. It was just for the sake of feeling their bodies together, connected. His rocking movements were tender and languid, savoring and sweet. Andy thought to himself that he could spend all day just like this.

He was happier than he'd ever been in his life. He was in love with his best friend, and his best friend loved him back. The future suddenly seemed a lot more exciting.

Eventually, Wyatt lifted his head and gave him a goofy smile. "So, does this mean that I get to touch you all the time now? Not just during broadcasts?"

Andy laughed. "Yes, I give you permission to touch me anytime, day or night. And speaking of broadcasts," he glanced over at the laptop, "I have a feeling the fans are going apeshit right now."

Wyatt chuckled. "Yeah, we left them on a bit of cliffhanger, didn't we?"

"I can only imagine how many DMs I've got at this point." He bit his lip, "If you're comfortable with it, I think we should keep the channel going."

"Hmm," Wyatt scratched his chin thoughtfully, "Continue getting paid ridiculous amounts of money to have sex with you when I would be doing it for free anyway? Yeah, I think I'm comfortable with that." Andy laughed, and Wyatt kissed him again. Then his face changed, becoming suddenly shyer. "But, uh, I do have one request about that…"

"Of course. What is it?" Andy asked.

"When we finally do retire early and say goodbye to FanFrenzy," he looked down bashfully, running a thumb idly over Andy's cheek, "I want things between us to stay exclusive, even after it's all over."

Andy grinned. It was almost funny that Wyatt was acting as shy as he was when he was still sheathed inside him and had said that he loved him only moments before. "Is this your way of asking me to be your boyfriend?"

He flushed crimson and nodded.

Andy gently placed his hands on the sides of Wyatt's face and kissed him on the forehead. "Then, my answer is yes. From here on out, it's you and me."

Wyatt's face broke into a wide, joyous grin. He hugged Andy tightly and buried his face into the crook of his neck. When he spoke, his voice was muffled and thick with emotion, but the words were clear:

"It's you and me."

Epilogue

Two Years Later

"Ready?"

Wyatt turned to Andy with a reassuring smile. "Ready."

Andy nodded and logged into FanFrenzy. Today was their last broadcast. Their *actual* last broadcast. They'd officially been doing this for over two years, and they were ready to call it quits.

It was oddly bittersweet. Neither of them imagined that cam modeling would eventually become something meaningful and sentimental, but it had.

After Andy confessed his love for Wyatt on the air, their follower count surged again, and fans were waiting with bated breath to see how things would play out. For their following show, both Wyatt and Andy sat down and explained that they'd unexpectedly fallen in love with each other since they started filming. They went on to explain that neither of them was gay and that this was all very new to them. The fans were overwhelmingly supportive, and word quickly spread about the two straight bros who accidentally fell for each other. Three months after Andy let the truth about his feelings slip, they surpassed seventy-five thousand subscribers. Their viewership had continued to increase gradually since then.

Their broadcasts turned into video dairies. They'd update the fans on their latest adventures, answer their questions, and then, of course, have sex. Some fans stuck around to watch their relationship journey. Some just wanted to watch them fuck. Most were in it for both. It seemed that they had struck a perfect balance between hot and wholesome.

Since they'd officially become boyfriends, Andy started sleeping in Wyatt's bed. Andy's room, in turn, was transformed into a stage for their FanFrenzy shows. Andy still used the closet for his clothes, but otherwise, the space was mostly occupied by cameras and lights and microphones and an absurd number of sex toys. It was no longer a cozy place to sleep at night. But that was fine because Wyatt didn't mind sharing his bed in the slightest. In fact, he preferred it that way.

Wyatt never went back to his old job. He did FanFrenzy full-time with Andy and managed their finances. They decided on a generous monthly allowance for themselves, and Wyatt put the rest of their earnings into savings and IRAs and ETFs and CDs and other acronyms that meant nothing to Andy. God, he was lucky to have Wyatt. Funny enough, Wyatt thought the same thing about him. While finances came easily to him, he knew he didn't have the same natural charisma that Andy brought to their audience. He maintained that Andy was the secret ingredient to their online success (though, Andy would adamantly deny it).

Thanks to several spreadsheets and razor-sharp financial planning, they'd reached their early retirement goals and were set monetarily for life. Of course, they both planned to find jobs eventually in the future, but it would be motivated by personal interest, not necessity. Andy had a dream of opening a climbing gym somewhere—maybe abroad—with walls suitable for all ages and experience levels. This was a far-off dream for the time being, however. Right now, the only thing they cared about was enjoying their retirement, and that meant traveling.

They'd mapped out an itinerary for the next eight months to travel throughout Europe and Asia. For the first six weeks, Leslie would be joining them. She'd become good friends with both of the boys over the years. Shortly after they started dating, Wyatt got a membership at Fitness 365 and received personal training sessions with Andy. Leslie had been just as tough on Wyatt in the gym as she had been on Andy, but the results were undeniable. They were both in the best shape of their lives.

Leslie's boyfriend, Cameron, would *not* be joining them on their travels, because he was now her *ex*-boyfriend. Leslie never went into the full details as to what happened between them. Andy had gleaned that something strange had happened between him and his boss. Something that might've been intimate? It didn't make much sense, but clearly, the relationship hadn't ended on good terms. Even so, that was months ago now and she was ready to go out and find herself "a hunky Italian man."

All three of them were excited to travel. Their flight was a week from today, and Andy and Wyatt were already packed. First things first, though, they had to say goodbye to the FanFrenzy family.

Andy started the broadcast and gave a wave to the camera.

"Hey, everyone. Today's show is a bittersweet one. It marks the end of a very special chapter of our relationship journey, as well as the beginning of something new and exciting. We're saying goodbye to FanFrenzy."

Already, messages were pouring in from fans, expressing their heartbreak but also their support. Andy and Wyatt had hinted weeks ago that they were thinking of stepping away from their account, so it wasn't coming as a complete shock, but it was obvious that many people were still genuinely sad to say farewell.

To his surprise, Andy found himself getting quietly emotional about saying goodbye to everyone. He swallowed around the small lump in his throat, and Wyatt reached over and laced his fingers in his. Andy turned to him and smiled, finding immediate solace in his soft blue eyes.

One username that was noticeably absent from the list of incoming messages was str8boyaddict. He (or she) had stopped tuning in to their show months ago. Their profile showed that they hadn't been online in ages. Andy sometimes wondered what happened to them, and he quietly hoped that everything was okay. Some part of him had secretly wished that they would be online for the final show because he wanted to thank them directly. None of this would've happened without them daring Andy to sneak into Wyatt's room in the first place. Str8boy unknowingly set everything into motion.

Andy was only a little disappointed that they hadn't shown. And as sad as it was to say goodbye, he couldn't deny that he was more excited than anything. The future stretched out ahead of them both like a red carpet, and Andy was eager to make the most of it.

Months ago, Andy bought a ring. Wyatt didn't know about it yet, but he would soon enough. Andy planned to propose on the final night of their travels. He'd asked Leslie if she thought it was a good idea, if she thought Wyatt would appreciate a romantic gesture like that. She'd given him a funny little smirk and told him that she was sure he would love it.

He'd never been more excited and nervous about anything in his life. He could hardly wait to pop the question, to spend the rest of his life with the man he loved, his best friend. God, he hoped he said yes…

Little did he know that Wyatt also had a ring secretly stowed away in his luggage.

———

Thank you so much for reading!

If you enjoyed this story, be on the lookout for the next installment in the Gay Awakenings series—The Secret Lives of CEOs—*which will tell the story of Cameron Thompson (Leslie's ex), another straight boy who develops an intense relationship with his domineering new boss, Maxwell Renaud. This novel should be out later in 2022 or early 2023!*

In the meantime, please feel free to check out my other works:

The Art of Desire

Tonight Belongs to Us

To receive occasional emails regarding new releases, sign up for my mailing list here! -
https://sendfox.com/joeymayble

Made in the USA
Columbia, SC
22 December 2024